The Bandit

&

His King

Richard Crowley

Order this book online at www.trafford.com
or email orders@trafford.com

Most Trafford titles are also available at major online book retailers.

Printed in Victoria, BC, Canada.

ISBN: 978-1-4269-1983-1

*Our mission is to efficiently provide the world's finest, most
comprehensive book publishing service, enabling every author to
experience success. To find out how to publish your book, your way, and
have it available worldwide, visit us online at www.trafford.com*

Trafford rev. 11/16/2009

www.trafford.com

North America & international
toll-free: 1 888 232 4444 (USA & Canada)
phone: 250 383 6864 ♦ fax: 812 355 4082

One

Unforgivable. That's what it was. how a man who dreamed of the stars could spend his days pushing a dirt father. The sun was heavy as the few rocky escarpments that showed up in the wastelands of the Northern climes. Anon, a person of no means, had to live on the sweat of his brow if he was to get any living whatsoever. The sun baked and fried the pale sand and blistered and reddened his arms, neck and shoulders. Anon looked heavenward to see if there was any way of escaping the sun's wrath. Alas there was no respite in his imagination as well as the bright yellow sky devoid entirely of sheltering clouds or storms. He could have used a drenching downpour art about this time. He would rather drown in tepid water than to be baked alive in this wilderness that he called his home.

Only the creeping vines loved the sun and they showed their joy in it by sending forth new, bright-green tendrils that walked silently across the land in search of water and any form of soil depression to start a new plant that would repeat the process until the weather changed or it was plucked from thence by a diligent farmer.

This man was no such farmer. He relished the sight of these self-sustaining creepers. They reminded him of his own life: a life among thorns, constantly jamming his hydraulic spade into soil so hard that even the hardest of metals would buckle under its pressure. Wiping the sweat from his brow, Anon looked longingly toward the bright blue sky that stretch from forever in the West to forever again in the East. The real show would come at night when he saw the height of the stars, the majesty of them, and heard the creatures of the night worshipping there, too. The night was a symphony. Everywhere animals crawled from the safety of the daylong homes and into the night hunting for anything that might resemble food: here a cricket, there a voracious beetle and the tender edges of the vine growth. "non sat in the dust and marveled at the creation. Surely the spectacle was made for him and him alone. Anon looked deeper into the skies and saw a life that he wanted. All by himself, he would ply the trade lines of the civilized systems mining for gold and iridium on derelict asteroids that careened this way and that.

Anon curiously poked at these vines wondering how they could thrive in such bleak conditions. They were purple and covered almost entirely by thorns. Poisonous spiders often sought shelter beneath a thicket of them as "non had sadly found out. It was a tale he often dwelt on as he scraped through the hardened ground. His life, he decided, was like that scrub vine.

There was so much to learn. He had heard stories of mysterious men in strange "star tractors" that landed in abandoned fields, took samples of the soil created impressions on the rock-hard sand and then sped off as soon as they had come. Anon knew these stories to be true because he had seen the depressions in the dirt with his own eye and, before they were covered by creeping vines, he could see the outlandish markings of a foot that was clearly not of Saurian origin. What would become of Saurus, he wondered. Why should I care, he thought angrily. I will travel among the stars in a tractor. My tractor will be the best and fastest in the galaxy.

The thoughts warmed "non's spirit and he quickly finished up his work and walked home with a spring in his step. All the world seemed to flower with the intense brilliance. Scrub trees that seemed to droop and languish all day long came alive in the night and "non's dreams only made them seem to dance and sway to an inaudible tune. Miles and miles of open trails seemed as nothing to him as he gazed upward to the stars that grew more active and more magical by the instant. "non regretted that he had to open and shut the door of his mean cottage and sleep until the light of the morning. The stars had awoken him.

Two

"Oops, er...damn. Not another one. "There's just no end of 'em."

"What's that Raf? "" female voice rose from a speaker on the dash.

"It's these Kweegons/Visitors, whatever, We fed them last month and here they are again 'cept now, there's more of them! Climbing all over the scanners like they were maggots or something."

Patsy looked at the visual screen and studied the undulating images of dozens of the organic crafts for a moment. The image was not impressive to her as she gazed into the stars for something that they could not give: an end to the ceaseless boredom of policing the scene of the most barren part of the "So many of them. Must have 'morphed, Raf. Who cares? I'm tired" Patsy leaned back in her chair at the navigation bar and ran her fingernails along the soft mesh fabric of the armrests on her seat.

Patsy largely ignored the ravings of her immediate scouting partner, Rafael Jack, and chose instead to spend hours at a time gazing at stars and planets as they traveled their courses across that which was called "charted space." She envisaged herself as a sort of goldfish in a vast pool of swirling water too massive and so filthy with ambition and greed to comprehend and she liked it that way. Survey life was a drag. So was recording every little thing that happened on a dreary day. If anything, she welcomed the aliens and they peril their presence brought. It was a pedestrian job to ply the stars in search of more or less intelligent life. She, as a result, refused to become one with her profession The Mon Ami, a scout ship and member of the third survey of the Outer.

The kweegons were a race of what seemed to be psychic beings. Always hungry for food or minds to snack on, they roamed the outer reaches and sometimes became the unwelcome addition to an ill-equipped survey shuttle. Once infected, a ship's crew could not remove the infestation of such creatures until docking at a major facility. Visitors were the bane of the Igoilenat.

Once established on a ship, the creatures had the ability to probe the mind's eye of each and every person until the order and trajectory of the ship was changed from that of a survey ship to that of a colony for future generations of Visitors. Every Igoilenat captain could point to the loss of a loved one for the purpose of creating more instances of the Visitor Hive process. But the Igoilenat were learning.

The Mon Ami was the first of a new breed of shuttles that included rudimentary psi-shielding in walls, crew stations, lavatories and the research deck. Naturally, larger ships were fitted with more robust psi-shielding, but simple shuttle craft like those of the survey teams were still very vulnerable and neglected. Patsy viewed the matter with nonchalance while Rafael was forever panicking at the least indication of any one of their species.

"I'm calling up Radinon. Soon we can get out of here," he said in a quivering voice.

"Radinon check. N"V Check. "auto dispersal is engaged," Patsy replied as she attended the bar. Raf, Look at this. They're still coming-in larger numbers!"

"C'mon Radinon. What the hell is wrong with this briefcase?" He said referring to the ship's mainframe. "I could've counted my way out by now"

"Easy Raf" Came Patsy's calm voice, "Just starting Transmittal now".

Three

Radinon was an aging program, but it had served the outland colonies well. Radinon was free to use and was robust as a main navigator program as well as an operating system for a number of compatible mainframes. "s fate would have it, the Mon Ami was fitted with a Radinon 1 on the 40dx30 ship's deck, the most modern of the older communication servers, but the oldest of deck configurations. Radinon, in all of its iterations, was a staple in nearly every moderately advanced settlement of the Outer worlds. The Mon Ami had skirted certain doom through the use of the very pedestrian program many times before. But now the minds of the Visitors had been on the move again. By inhabiting the minds of the users, the Visitors could easily break through some setups and slow down or infect others. Patsy learned early in her naval career that an intimate relation to Radinon meant the success or failure of an entire operation not to mention the lives of the crew. The colonies were filled with minds laid waste by the parasites. Living breathing, vacuous persons with no will to live or desire for normal pleasures. Those were indeed the dead zones of the universe and Patsy had the Visitors and incompetent navigational officers to blame. Inside, she burned with anger at this, but her outward countenance only showed boredom and disregard for all things naval and scout-related. Would that Rafael would act the same, she thought, then we could fight these predators toe-to-ganglion.

While Patsy mused, Rafael perspired and obsessed over the dashboard looking for yet other ways to survey without coming across the accursed creatures.

"Looks like we have our hands full, this time" Patsy groaned, "they're still getting through and Radinon is not stopping them." Patsy and Rafael knew of no other remedy. Complete total shutdown was needed. "s Yellow-green light flooded the cavernous walkways and console rooms of Mon Ami, Patsy breathed heavily and Rafael lay back in his chair in thoughtful rest. They both knew that Visitors could not penetrate a dead ship. After all, dead ships hold no minds and thus no food or lodging for a new colony. Several of the approaching aliens already carried ships of their own. Their feeding frenzies had drawn them to consume entire crews and shipboard computers.

Rafael and Patsy saw the remains of ships from vastly diverse ends of the galaxy" Andilaxians, Xerxian pendili and even the more humanoid Raakish Tsetercraft had been attacked and assimilated into an ever-widening hive that now stretched between several of the approaching alien craft. Clearly they wanted the meager shuttle as an afterthought to round out the day's meal

"s Mon Ami halted all of its systems, it ebbed and flowed from the gravitic center of the craft and a nearby moon occupied by a Igoilenat mining corporation. Rafael wished he could crash the shuttle just to get away from the Visitors, butter doing so would invite their wrath upon the innocent company of miners and destroy whatever social fabric that occupied the place.

"No," Patsy said," "We'll have to keep this up for the next three days-floating and listing like a dead animal."

"Which is not far from where we were before," Rafael said as he pounded the console with a partially opened fist.

When the Visitors came, it was to a ship that looked deserted of life forms. Only a scout crew came aboard testing the hallways and electronic makeup of the ship. Patsy and Rafael had locked themselves in an antechamber of the sickbay and remained quiet and calm. The Visitors found them, just as they had found thousands and even millions of sentient beings before.

The low-grade psi-shielding of the sick bay was meant to protect wounded surveyors security crewman and general staff from being affected by outside effects of psionic radiation that emanated from some environments and locales. Now, the same system failed to shield Patsy and Rafael from the probing minds of the Visitors. Slowly and almost robotically, the two crawled from their place of hiding and submitted themselves to the unwelcome guests.

"stone-faced Patricia returned to her place at the navigation bar while a zombie of what appeared walked to the dashboard. Under an unseen control, the team of two surrendered the results of more than ten years of interstellar survey work. It was clear what the Visitors wanted-something to hide their presence in the systems outside Home and to further entice victims into their psychic nets. Patsy and Rafael were only a pair of the latest victims from Home to stray into the matrix of the Visitors. Like others, Patsy and Rafael became shadows of their former selves, eternally perched at the controls of a ship they once guided. In months, muscles tightened creating garish agonized expressions on the faces of the explorers as they were carried along on the back of old prey. The scene was historic. Skeletons of craft clung to other craft of entirely different origin. The Mon Ami was conjoined to a Andilaxian ship's boat which in turn was met with a more primitive ship. It was only the non-shielded craft that became easy prey. Modern craft that sported full shielding had nearly complete control over the chance encounters with Kweegons.

Home depended on the freewheeling exploits of star messengers to remedy the all too often loss of cargo, robbing of pleasure craft and hijacking of shuttle craft.

The bounty hunters arose out of the central system to remedy and repel the action of privateering ships. It was they, after all, who made the scouting missions possible and they who allowed system craft to operate in safety.

Oteph Black was one of a fine order of mongrel space travelers. Though his trade ship's cramped quarters, it had been shielded within and without with the highest quality of repellent in or out of the shady sectors of the universe. Oteph also wore clothing consisting of a dark tunic, thick gloves and a snug fitting hat that had a small visor. His vessel plied the fringes of the outer worlds where the hijackings.

Oteph hadn't heard of the Mon Ami an didn't care. It was an Andilaxian heavy cruiser that whetted his appetite for foreign money.

"s pristine as the day that she was taken, the cruiser hung clung helplessly to a what seemed a vast pile of metal debris. Indeed, the Visitors had been known to feed on the very things that were inedible or wasteful to other species. How perfect it was, then, that Oteph should happen upon such a tribe of people as devoted to surfeiting as he was.

Within two hours of his boarding of the Andilaxus-type tub, as he had now dubbed it, he felt the need to graze. "quick look through the craft revealed a galley that could have served twelve officers or seaman in reasonably comfortable. Old food stores, rotted with age, lined the deep shelves of a once-productive mess hall. How fortunate! The food stores aboard the Salvulent had grown bland and out-of-date and here, in a derelict was not only a complete dining facility but also a

Well, I guess I'm not that hungry, Oteph thought. He strode softly through the powdery dust that clung to the floor and eventual fixed itself to the base of his boots. The survey shuttle consisted of two main thoroughfares, 4 state rooms and a scientific lab. When Oteph reached the bridge to see the former crew members crumpled over the control panels with garish expressions on their long-dead faces, he was confirmed in his mind that the mind manipulators had been here.

The remainder of the ship was covered in the strange white powder and Oteph feared that he himself might become a permanent resident as the powder turned to a gray, syrupy glue that made movement difficult and built up on the treads of his boot soles. Soon, all of the white powder took on the grayish color and that which had collected on the walls made the corridors seem like caverns made of fly paper.

"s a pirate, Oteph saw himself as smarter than most space travelers that plied cruisers, yachts and even other snub craft. He fashioned baking plates to the bottoms of his boots and, as he slid slowly from passageway to access duct, he reached the airlock, none the wiser concerning the strange ship, its dead bodies and the mercurial paste that seem to grow in strength as he remained aboard and wandered the corridors of the dead survey ship.

Oteph's own craft, the Salvulent B, was a snub craft or small freight carrier. Long ago, the pilots of such carriers were branded with some accuracy, to be pirates. Oteph was one of them. If he could not find live merchant ships to plunder, he robbed the decrepit ships left hollowed by the Visitors. This, then was the Mon Ami, his "Andilaxus, the ship of the hour. The trick was to get it free of the muck of the Visitors' traveling junkyard and then to see what riches could be found in the computers and the ship's stores. Surveyors often held twice the provisions of standard cruisers and most held highly valuable scientific equipment.

There was little that could be done for the infestation of the gray paste. He first tried burning it, scraping at the charred remains and then finally he used an electrolysis kit from the Salvulent to physically separate the remains from the doors, computers , controls and dashboards of the craft. Within a week, he had cleaned most of the ship and began painting the insides with psychic shielding in hopes that the temporary fix would allow a quiet escape from the mind leeching Kweegons, as his fathers had called them.

Filthy beggars, he heard a voice in his head say. Only try to take things from helpless people that don't know better. Damnable race, if you can call them that, the voice continued. Probably some still aboard. No worries, he thought. Such thoughts were part of the life he gloried in.

Oteph rested his hand confidently on the hilt of his cold flag. Down a corridor, he heard a scurrying sound like sharp claws clattering across a metal floor. In a moment they were gone and then such a howling and screeching sound filled the air that his ears, though tightly wrapped inside his cap felt as though they would burst. He felt himself slipping away from reality. He fell against the wall and slowly sank onto the cold metal plates that served as floorboards for the ship. The last thing he remembered was watching helplessly while a short fair-skinned creature poked him with sharp little metal sticks.

It seemed like days until Oteph found himself awake and plastered to the floor by gray slime. His joints were sore and his jaw ached. His psi-shielding suit was gone as was his visor. Oteph looked down the corridor of the ship call Mon Ami and saw that it was still lifeless and empty. But it wasn't true. Someone was here, he thought. Without a psychic shield for his body he was vulnerable from any kind of attack. Oteph had heavyset, brutish features, but his mind was weak and only knew the ways of hand-to-hand combat. The only recourse to get to the Salvulent or to race to the infirmary. He remembered that old ships carried minimal psi-shielding in their sickbays. Thus, he quickly struggled to lift himself and hobble down the corridor on his bare feet that stung with every step on the cold metal floor.

The sick bay of the Mon Ami was little more than just a stripped down room with about ten bunks, neuro-sensing machines and a central rack of laser-enhanced surgical implements. Oteph sought refuge under one of the bunks but found that his belly could not fit where his head and feet so easily could. Quickly he searched the room for a place to hide. "n empty medicine locker seemed a good choice until the rotted corpse of a former crew member fell out in pieces on the floor at his feet. Taken aback, Oteph grabbed an ID tag from the midst of the grisly husk. It was a picture ID for the Imperial Survey Command, an auxiliary for the Home Imperial Navy. The picture had long faded away, but the name and rank written on the card was that of Machinist First Class R. Jack. Oteph crouched inside the locker while he heard the familiar scuttling sounds from outside the door. He felt like vulnerable and it was then that realized that physical strength like his would be nothing compared to the psychic powers that laid waste the minds of the crew turning the Mon Ami into a ghost ship.

During his lengthy stay in the prison-like medical bay, Oteph fashioned a turban out of a roll of extra heavy cerebral gauze that he had coated in what he thought was cardiac protecting grease. He had hoped that the crudely constructed cap would serve as a psi-shield long enough for him to reach to hatch of his own craft. Oteph counted off the hours when the scurrying creatures were active and what seemed to be their inactive or perhaps rest times. Carefully he crept out of the sick bay and into the main corridor. There was only a few yards to traverse until he would come to the exit panel and then the airlock. Oteph used his highly developed hearing ability to detect motion from the farthest regions of the small ship. Everything seemed OK. Oteph walked haltingly and close to the floor hoping he would not be set upon. But his precautions were of no use. He soon found himself face to face with a gaggle of the creatures. They were humanoid in form with pale, almost white skin and gentle bluish hair. Oteph was at once taken in by their beauty and then realized that he was yet the victim of another trap. Kweegons were a repulsive race with green, hairless hide and characteristic wart patterns. Oteph gazed deeply at one of them that he thought to be their leader and sure enough, the comely appearance of the faded to reveal a most disgusting green snout with a protruding eyes that seem to burn in their sockets. The young kweegon had green skin and covered itself with protective slime which seemed to flow across the creature's skin as Oteph held its gaze. It seemed as though time had stopped while he looked at the creatures.

Oteph, sensing an unseen threat and anger in the air, rested the chuff of his hand on the knob of his electro-flag, a silly weapon that he affectionately called "the whip of Doom." The visitors would have to move first before the fat, battle-hardened corsair would draw his weapon. He silently gloated to himself over the superiority that he felt over the disgusting little creatures The leader of the group sensed his anger at once and, as a company, the Kweegons seemed to concentrate their mental powers.

"There is no help for you, space urchin. Turn back or die, they seemed to say. Flee to your ship, it will not avail you. We own you now just as this pitiable ship. Prepare to meet its divine wreckage."

Oteph acted without thinking. Spinning his flag from its holster, he slashed his way through the crowd of short beings, blooding the floor with each kweegon that he hit. The creatures scattered except for a tall gray one in the back who looked at Oteph with a sort of humorous interest. Quickly he grabbed the long whip in his long tentacled fingers and reeled in Oteph as if he were some kind of Homely sea-beast. Oteph let go of the flag just as he became an arm's length away from the creature. The electrically charged handle flipped from his hand and smashed into the elderly creature's face and green steaming blood flowed from the leader's face.

"Hah! Learned that from the Saurians-sector fifty!" The old creature smiled as he wrapped the whip around his fingers and fastened it into oval wreath. He placed the impromptu crown on his head and beamed at the now shocked pirate.

"You see much, young one, but not enough." He began, " We mean to cleanse this universe. And you with it. You interest me. Why do you steal what you can never keep, Little Monster?"

Oteph was flabbergasted. Never had he been referred to in such a manner. "I rule this universe, green hag, this is my turf. And my turf-you don't surf! There's nothing you can do about it." Oteph smiled to himself about his witty comeback

The angry reaction pleased the gentle alien.

"Come, now, Monster, join us or join the wreckage. You'll come to it eventually. Patsy and Rafael couldn't stop it and neither can you. My name is Thaulab. I can help you, fat Monster. Join with us and we can rule the galaxy."

The strange mellifluous tones of the Kweegon's voice was pleasing to Oteph and he felt himself slipping into a reverie even as the alien spoke to him. The trance was short-lived, though as Oteph glared back at the green and gray alien.

"Thaulab, if you ever get by me you'll always be a poor parasite-never creating, always grazing. Join the Salvulent. Join me, I'll show you into these pathetic civilizations.

Home is a poor excuse for a planet and yet you want to feed on them. This place where we stand, the height of their scientific genius. Bah! The Saurians and I were doing the survey routes 80 millennia ago and in bigger ships. Neutron drives! Quintillian shielding!" As Oteph maneuvered his rotund body in dramatic fashion to express what he thought was insurmountable reason, the old alien looked tired and wheezed as he rested his chin on his slender chest.

"Finished? OK. So, you claim your ship is fast?"

"Darn straight it's fast. Faster than this flying garbage dump, anyway."

Thaulab turned his back to Oteph and began gathering together his small group of bruised, bloodied and humiliated followers. Moments passed before they turned again to Oteph." Realizing that Oteph's species were not psychically aligned, the little once spoke to him in turn in soft gentle sound combinations, "Oh, round one, fret not the loss of your life and that of this. The Igoilenat race and yours will be ours."

Four

Suddenly, Oteph felt a profound knowledge of things inside and outside of himself. He saw the Mon Ami as the ship's computer would see it, all at once and neatly files into cascades of data. Radinon, the formidable ship's defense mechanism was but a small afterthought to him. Generations of Igoilenat survey work-and that of its former crew were made real. The all-seeing knowledge was too much, at first. The kweegons looked and laughed as they saw him covering his head and falling to the floor. For Oteph, the world darkened and passed away. His body rebelled. Muscles and joints, myelin sheaths dissolved in an instant from the basest parts of his brain. The result was a seizure that nearly killed him. Cardio and pulmonary systems shut down almost completely as he reeled from the shock and he thrashed about the floor and finally became still, face purple and bleeding from the mouth where he had bitten a good portion of his tongue off. The kweegons were quick to react. Younger ones applied their small tentacled hands to his seemingly lifeless form while Thaulab and the elders meditated.

Oteph woke to find himself in the familiar confines of the Mon Ami's sick bay. Firm straps held him firmly to the cot and a protective jaw guard kept his mouth stationary while Thaulab, looking taller and more compassionate than usual, looked down on him.

"You must learn to embrace the light, my friend not resist it," he talked as though he was reading out of a book, "Your primitive mind cannot grasp the complexity of the psychic communication that you must learn. We'll start with Radinon. You'll learn every inch of that program before the week is out and you'll be tested."

Oteph tried to respond, but found that the protective harness and bit prevented him from moving his jaw or even the angle of his head.

"You will start with Patricia I Buonaparte. She programmed the current version and a study of her thought files will assist you in learning the basic outlay of the mechanism."

Oteph stared at his partner with keen interest that was seasoned with a genuine fear of the shipboard computer. He knew nothing of computers and much less about talking to them. "All of his life he had concerned himself with petty theft, hijacking and hand-to-and combat-the virtues of life. Comp-jockeys were miscreants, miserable, lonely lost souls that lived a life of homage to machine and science. He sniffed at the proposal of studying the life of one of the 'greats' of the Igoilenat Space Navigating Society.

"Well, you're in it now, fat Monster," Thaulab seemed to have sensed his thoughts directly, "You are our last hope against the Igoilenat. Radinon is only the least of their defenses. They have more-you'll see, you will see."

But the Salvulent, Oteph thought. It's fast. It's complex...

You're right. The Salvulent is a pirate ship, meant for shooting and boarding. What're you going to do? Throw a wrench at them; crash through an airlock that you don't know exists? You're hungry. Come. Eat."

Five

The off watches of the night were spent with the creatures of the hive and Oteph grew to love the life-giving aura that pervaded the galley as new kweegons were hatched almost every day. Often, he just sat in a chair and marveled at the process of a new life being created from what he saw as nothing. Life seemed to engender itself as he watched. Sure, there was the odd occasion when the hive needed protein for food, but the marvel of the hive was its never ending fecundity. Oteph learn to respect and enjoy the fellowship of the other kweegons aboard the ship. Thaulab soon took him under his wise confidence and set out to teach Oteph the ways of the mind readers.

"It's easy once you think of it," he would say to Oteph's amazement. In time Oteph learned the basics of the kweegon lifestyle and learned to control his feelings of uncontrollable rage. Oteph began to consider a life that was not possible before. Thaulab often sat beside him while watched the hive and Tovalu and the others piloted the Regiceld deeper into the territory of the Igoilenat.

"What do you think of them, Oteph," Thaulab asked with a gleam in his eye.

"I think they're marvelous. Toiling here day after day without a friend or cultivator near."

"Soon you will know that freedom, my friend."

Oteph looked at his new master and then turned back to the hive as it repeated its soft methodical vibration over and over again.

So this was life. Oteph had not known life since he had left his home on Saurus. There the sun beat down on every inch of soil and only cooled when it was invisible for the brief periods of night. All that and Saurian life and culture depended on the reclamation of the wastelands overgrown with gnarled woods and choking vines. But the hive was different. Here, life made itself anew every time he look upon its pulsating orbs. Newborn kweegons were simply the embodiment of health and fecundity. Oteph marveled, but Thaulab simply looked on with pride and satisfaction. Oteph felt his energy and it was profoundly blessed.

Six

With each passing day, the kweegons grew more attached and amused with their prisoner. Oteph, however, needed twice the amount of food as usual to keep up his laborious studies of the former crew of the Mon Ami. Patricia I and her whilom first mate, Rafael, had modified the electrical controls of the ship in anticipation of an attack by the Visitors. If not for his outright hatred of what he called electronic meddlers, he would have had to admit their genius.

The ship's navigation program, the Radinon 2.0.0.1 was a modification that allowed minimal psi-shielding in certain decks and parts of the computer. Patricia I modified the code to include remote airlock control for the prevention of pirate raids (Oteph sniffed at the idea), cosmic billowing and vagrant particle rays. In short, Radinon-Patricia functioned closer to the fashion of a human brain than had all low-tech low-budget computers of its time. The one called Patsy knew of the dangers of the Outer and the vulnerability of her own race. Oteph grew stronger as he perused millions of lines of code simply to learn the process of automatic laundry indicators, a system that had also been subjected to redesign and "Innovations." Patricia I's addition's to the system's code was simply the complete and total linkage of every single ship function to a single dashboard. " long-winded determination of the vital versus the mundane in the ship's life. The difference was huge. Instead of a defenseless scientific scout vessel, the Mon Ami was a travelling center of protected life.

In spite of his growing knowledge of the kweegon method of life, Oteph was still muted from the loss of his tongue. Depression set in as he slowly thought about the possibility of a life without riches. "life without weapons. The Kweegons, after all, didn't value objects, just the minds and souls of the things that inhabited them. The Raison d'être of kweegon life was the body politic just as it was the action of feeding on the thoughts of others.

"We are legion," a smiling Thaulab would often say to his new apprentice. The system eventually made sense to him. The Kweegons needed the Mon Ami in order to complete a mass consumption of the Igoilenat race and the system called by them, Home.

Soon he learned to communicate through signs and psychic projections. Thaulab and his others aided the addled pirated by supporting him through vast amounts of food, mental comfort and tight physical constraint. Oteph became used to being held to a chair while his mouth and head were immobilized. He was finally ready to investigate the vanilla version of Radinon, the version most common to the Andilaxian fleet operated by the Home worlders. From start to finish, Radinon was a standard interface to modify ship's temp, oxygen that was vital to the Igoilenat species and the rudimentary control of weapons, instruments and scientific explorations. Radinon was designed to go online just seconds before live beings entered the ship and maintain them through missions of up to one hundred years. After that, the computer would be expected to fail and the life forms with it. Large cruisers carried different coding that could perform different functions but never longer than a short hundred year period and never on a mere Andilaxian craft.

Long ago, engineers of the Andilax created short and long-range battle, survey and leisure craft. The computers that had long protected their creators had no need of change and thus coding remained unchanged for several millennia. By the time the Igoilenat reached space, Saurians, like

Oteph had long since developed and used craft with larger, faster power plants, more complex quintillian shielding systems and the neutron drive equation. Piracy was an art and those like Oteph were its aficionados. The primitive Saurians were gifted and powerful rulers of the space lanes, but the Andilaxian race soon developed highly secured vessels protected by the Radinon, a computerized environmental parsing system. I due time, the need for battle-ready and robust ship's operations became realized. Thus the name Radinon. Radinon Ng was the god of skies and fires, the creator of Andilaxus and its source of the creative. Radinon the computer was capable of both military and scientific application. "leisure edition operated on some yachts and controlled pleasure nodes and deck temperatures.

Rudimentary systems like the 0.9 line were installed on freighters and small barges. In time, Radinon developed into much more than a computer. When properly configured, Radinon equipped ships wore a stronger armor than any combat vessel known to the galaxy. They were the bane of Saurian and piratical livelihood. Until the time of the seconds, the Radinons soon fell victim to telepathic attacks by such psychic species.

The Mon Ami and the Salvulent continued on a direct course through Andilaxian space as Oteph and the crew studied the most basic of the Radinon computer structures. "s it happened, upon finding or being approached by a star ship outfitted with such a computer, The now studied computer director, Oteph would use a stock elude mechanism, the only one available on such an old ship. For their part, the Kweegons pooled their minds into defensive shields about the two docked ships. For days, Oteph gazed at the monitors until his eyes became sore.

"You must learn vigilance," Thaulab reminded him, "we are very close to danger. Very close."

"But if the Igoilenat attack we not only have this ship but also mine for the defense."

"My children have been playing with your toys and they won't be enough to fight against a superior craft of the modern Andilaxian Navy. I have fit your ship with new shielding and given an upgrade to the computer that should protect against computers up to the version 3."

"Excellent," Oteph laughed, "So you see, we'll just get in and get out and maybe take a few things as well. I heard that the Recipro have the highest tech numbers of any modern fleet outside of the Ng superstation."

Thaulab turned away from him and looked at a monitor on the vertical dashboard. Two ships approached. One of them was large like a sailing yacht and the other was small like an escort fighter. Together, they meant trouble. Thaulab rushed out of the bridge area and down the corridor to the galley where eighty of his kind sat and played relaxing games of cards and mental blocking.

"Pierre, Korg, Tuvalo. Come." At once three large beings rose from their chairs and followed Thaulab from the room. "although they bore many of the same features, the three Kweegons were decidedly different in aspect and facial appearance. Pierre, the tallest of the bunch, wore a short white beard that curled around his neck and nearly covered his snout. Korg, the shortest and fattest, wore spectacles always carried a bag of food with him. His body was nearly free of hair and his face was light green with large pink splotches. His tentacled fingers were also covered by a pink skin that indicated more of a disease than a racial characteristic. Strangely enough, they all came from the same planet

Tuvalo was tall, muscular and always sneered at those he met in corridors, along streets and in nearly every place that people met. His mannerisms were strange for a person who truly loved others and always looked for the best in those he met. Those who knew him, loved him and those who didn't were terrified to look at him.

"You're a pleasant book with a nasty cover," Thaulab used to chide. Tuvalo didn't care. It was up to him to save his dying race from the ever-expanding population of hominids that polluted the space that once belonged to his ancestors.

Oteph was a strange friend among such people. Being a hominid, he was hated, but being hated by other hominids made him a powerful ally. The Kweegons depended on him to guide system attacks against enemy computers. Only he knew how the Igoilenat configured their environmental controls. With his help, Thaulab and his family had successfully hijacked three older fighters and a cargo barge. Oteph was a quick study when it came to stealing things. Thaulab loved to see his hungry, lusty smile appear whenever the Andilaxian craft came into range.

"You want me ta go get 'em?" He would ask in his garbled, tongue-less speech. Thaulab would laugh within his mind at such things. We'll go far with this guy, he thought.

Thaulab stood vigilantly on the bridge with his three main officers and viewed that data screens that indicated the approach of the cruiser and its escort. Tuvalo held his fingers to his head as if to launch an attack on the ship.

"Belay that, Val," Thaulab said, "Let's invite them in. Oteph. Detach the barge."

Oteph did as he was told and watched as the large massive object began hurtling toward the cruiser that now seemed dwarfed by the size of the massive barge. "t first, the cruiser began to spin in an identical course away from the barge. Oteph quickly took control of the barge by running its physical plant through Mon Ami's Radinon. The cruiser shot rounds of reflective chaff to disorient the drive systems of the large ship, but when this didn't work, the barge was pelted by laser cannons from the cruiser. Finally, a slow flying torpedo finished off what was left of the barge.

"Let me at em, Thaulab," Oteph mumbled, "They can't dodge the Salvulent like that."

"Indeed they cannot, young pirate. And yet you cannot outlast their vigor."

The Mon-Ami continued its slow course into the Andilaxian region stopping only to recalibrate instruments thrown off by the accidental approach of the nearby Ng system.

The attacks came quickly. Out of nowhere, tiny cruisers surrounded the conglomeration of ships. Tuvalo was dispatched immediately to the Salvulent while Oteph and others of the kweegon crew operated the two smaller cruisers. Thaulab stayed behind in the Mon Ami to direct its movements and perhaps gain an edge over the leaner, smarter ships of the Ng empire. Even with Patricia I's creative developments to the Radinon 2, the Mon Ami lay naked against highly effective computer attacks while kweegon pilots and Oteph himself sought to draw fire away from their flagship, the broken-down survey ship. For hours, skillful piloting and creative thinking led the Ng corsairs away from the battle, but the success was short because the much newer ships bore complete psychic shielding and unbreakable computer systems. Thaulab pounded his flat hand against the dashboard as he saw his two ancient cruisers succumb to the superior abilities of the small defensive fleet of the Ng system. Of his two old cruisers, only one made it back to Mon Ami. Bleeding and clearly fatigued, Oteph blustered through the airlock slamming his large clumsy feet against either side of the walkway.

"They're too fast. Too many of 'em."

Seven

Oteph Black was one of a fine order of mongrel space travelers. Though his trade ship's cramped quarters, it had been shielded within and without with the highest quality of repellent in or out of the shady sectors of the universe. Oteph also wore clothing consisting of a dark tunic, thick gloves and a snug fitting hat that had a small visor. His vessel plied the fringes of the outer worlds where the hijackings.

Oteph hadn't heard of the Mon Ami an didn't care. It was an Andilaxian heavy cruiser that whetted his appetite for foreign money. "s pristine as the day that she was taken, the cruiser hung clung helplessly to a what seemed a vast pile of metal debris. Indeed, the Visitors had been known to feed on the very things that were inedible or wasteful to other species. How perfect it was, then, that Oteph should happen upon such a tribe of people as devoted to surfeiting as he was.

Within two hours of his boarding of the Andilaxus-type tub, as he had now dubbed it, he felt the need to graze. "quick look through the craft revealed a galley that could have served twelve officers or seaman in reasonably comfortable. Old food stores, rotted with age, lined the deep shelves of a once-productive mess hall. How fortunate! The food stores aboard the Salvulent had grown bland and out-of-date and here, in a derelict was not only a complete dining facility but also a

Well, I guess I'm not that hungry, Oteph thought. He strode softly through the powdery dust that clung to the floor and eventual fixed itself to the base of his boots. The survey shuttle consisted of two main thoroughfares, 4 state rooms and a scientific lab. When Oteph reached the bridge to see the former crew members crumpled over the control panels with garish expressions on their long-dead faces, he was confirmed in his mind that the mind manipulators had been here.

The remainder of the ship was covered in the strange white powder and Oteph feared that he himself might become a permanent resident as the powder turned to a gray, syrupy glue that made movement difficult and built up on the treads of his boot soles. Soon, all of the white powder took on the grayish color and that which had collected on the walls made the corridors seem like caverns made of fly paper.

"s a pirate, Oteph saw himself as smarter than most space travelers that plied cruisers, yachts and even other snub craft. He fashioned baking plates to the bottoms of his boots and, as he slid slowly from passageway to access duct, he reached the airlock, none the wiser concerning the strange ship, its dead bodies and the mercurial paste that seem to grow in strength as he remained aboard and wandered the corridors of the dead survey ship.

Oteph's own craft, the Salvulent B, was a snub craft or small freight carrier. Long ago, the pilots of such carriers were branded with some accuracy, to be pirates. Oteph was one of them. If he could not find live merchant ships to plunder, he robbed the decrepit ships left hollowed by the Visitors. This, then was the Mon Ami, his Andilaxus, the ship of the hour. The trick was to get it free of the muck of the Visitors' traveling junkyard and then to see what riches could be found in the computers and the ship's stores. Surveyors often held twice the provisions of standard cruisers and most held highly valuable scientific equipment.

There was little that could be done for the infestation of the gray paste. He first tried burning it, scraping at the charred remains and then finally he used an electrolysis kit from the Salvulent to physically separate the remains from the doors, computers , controls and dashboards of the craft. Within a week, he had cleaned most of the ship and began painting the insides with psychic shielding in hopes that the temporary fix would allow a quiet escape from the mind leeching Kweegons, as his fathers had described them while he was yet quite young and planet-bound in another star system.

"Filthy beggars," he heard a voice in his head say. Only try to take things from helpless people that don't know better. Damnable race, if you can call them that, the voice continued. Probably some still aboard. No worries, he thought. Such thoughts were part of the life he gloried in.

"Who's there?" Oteph called into the darkness. All that returned was a faint echo of his own voice, but the voices inside his head kept growing

He rested his hand confidently on the hilt of his cold flag. Down a corridor, he heard a scurrying sound like sharp claws clattering across a metal floor. In a moment they were gone and then such a howling and screeching sound filled the air that his ears, though tightly wrapped inside his cap felt as though they would burst. He felt himself slipping away from reality. He fell against the wall and slowly sank onto the cold metal plates that served as floorboards for the ship. The last thing he remembered was watching helplessly while a short fair-skinned creature poked him with sharp little metal sticks.

It seemed like days until Oteph found himself awake and plastered to the floor by gray slime. His joints were sore and his jaw ached. His psi-shielding suit was gone as was his visor. Oteph looked down the corridor of the ship call Mon Ami and saw that it was still lifeless and empty. But it wasn't true. Someone was here, he thought. Without a psychic shield for his body he was vulnerable from any kind of attack. Oteph had heavyset, brutish features, but his mind was weak and only knew the ways of hand-to-hand combat. The only recourse to get to the Salvulent or to race to the infirmary. He remembered that old ships carried minimal psi-shielding in their sickbays. Thus, he quickly struggled to lift himself and hobble down the corridor on his bare feet that stung with every step on the cold metal floor.

The sick bay of the Mon Ami was little more than just a stripped down room with about ten bunks, neuro-sensing machines and a central rack of laser-enhanced surgical implements. Oteph sought refuge under one of the bunks but found that his belly could not fit where his head and feet so easily could. Quickly he searched the room for a place to hide. "n empty medicine locker seemed a good choice until the rotted corpse of a former crew member fell out in pieces on the floor at his feet. Taken aback, Oteph grabbed an ID tag from the midst of the grisly husk. It was a picture ID for the Imperial Survey Command, an auxiliary for the Home Imperial Navy. The picture had long faded away, but the name and rank written on the card was that of Machinist First Class R. Jack. Oteph crouched inside the locker while he heard the familiar scuttling sounds from outside the door. He felt like vulnerable and it was then that realized that physical strength like his would be nothing compared to the psychic powers that laid waste the minds of the crew turning the Mon Ami into a ghost ship.

During his lengthy stay in the prison-like medical bay, Oteph fashioned a turban out of a roll of extra heavy cerebral gauze that he had coated in what he thought was cardiac protecting grease. He had hoped that the crudely constructed cap would serve as a psi-shield long enough for him to reach to hatch of his own craft. Oteph counted off the hours when the scurrying creatures were active and what seemed to be their inactive or perhaps rest times. Carefully he crept out of the sick bay and into the main corridor. There was only a few yards to traverse until he would come to the exit panel and then the airlock. Oteph used his highly developed hearing ability to detect motion from the farthest regions of the small ship. Everything seemed OK. Oteph walked haltingly and close to the floor hoping he would not be set upon. But his precautions were of no use. He soon found himself face to face with a gaggle of the creatures. They were humanoid in form with pale, almost white skin and gentle bluish hair. Oteph was at once taken in by their beauty and then realized that he was yet the victim of another trap. Kweegons were a repulsive race with green, hairless hide and characteristic wart patterns. Oteph gazed deeply at one of them that he thought to be their leader and sure enough, the comely appearance of the faded to reveal a most disgusting green snout with a protruding eyes that seem to burn in their sockets. The young kweegon had green skin and covered itself with protective slime which seemed to flow across the creature's skin as Oteph held its gaze. It seemed as though time had stopped while he looked at the creatures.

Oteph, sensing an unseen threat and anger in the air, rested the chuff of his hand on the knob of his electro-flag, a silly weapon that he affectionately called "the whip of Doom." The visitors would have to move first before the fat, battle-hardened corsair would draw his weapon. He silently gloated to himself over the superiority that he felt over the disgusting little creatures The leader of the group sensed his anger at once and, as a company, the Kweegons seemed to concentrate their mental powers.

"There is no help for you, space urchin. Turn back or die, they seemed to say. Flee to your ship, it will not avail you. We own you now just as this pitiable ship. Prepare to meet its divine wreckage."

Oteph acted without thinking. Spinning his flag from its holster, he slashed his way through the crowd of short beings, blooding the floor with each kweegon that he hit. The creatures scattered except for a tall gray one in the back who looked at Oteph with a sort of humorous interest. Quickly he grabbed the long whip in his long tentacled fingers and reeled in Oteph as if he were some kind of Homely sea-beast. Oteph let go of the flag just as he became an arm's length away from the creature. The electrically charged handle flipped from his hand and smashed into the elderly creature's face and green steaming blood flowed from the leader's face.

"Hah! Learned that from the Saurians-sector fifty!" The old creature smiled as he wrapped the whip around his fingers and fastened it into oval wreath. He placed the impromptu crown on his head and beamed at the now shocked pirate.

"You see much, young one, but not enough." He began, " We mean to cleanse this universe. And you with it. You interest me.

Why do you steal what you can never keep, Little Monster?"

Oteph was flabbergasted. Never had he been referred to in such a manner. "I rule this universe, green hag, this is my turf. And my turf-you don't surf! There's nothing you can do about it." Oteph smiled to himself about his witty comeback

The angry reaction pleased the gentle alien.

"Come, now, Monster, join us or join the wreckage. You'll come to it eventually. Patsy and Rafael couldn't stop it and neither can you. My name is Thaulab. I can help you, fat Monster. Join with us and we can rule the galaxy."

The strange mellifluous tones of the Kweegon's voice was pleasing to Oteph and he felt himself slipping into a reverie even as the alien spoke to him. The trance was short-lived, though as Oteph glared back at the green and gray alien.

"Thaulab, if you ever get by me you'll always be a poor parasite-never creating, always grazing. Join the Salvulent. Join me, I'll show you into these pathetic civilizations. Home is a poor excuse for a planet and yet you want to feed on them. This place where we stand, the height of their scientific genius. Bah! The Saurians and I were doing the survey routes 80 millennia ago and in bigger ships. Neutron drives! Quintillian shielding!" As Oteph maneuvered his rotund body in dramatic fashion to express what he thought was insurmountable reason, the old alien looked tired and wheezed as he rested his chin on his slender chest.

"Finished? OK. So, you claim your ship is fast?"

"Darn straight it's fast. Faster than this flying garbage dump, anyway."

Thaulab turned his back to Oteph and began gathering together his small group of bruised, bloodied and humiliated followers. Moments passed before they turned again to Oteph." Realizing that Oteph's species were not psychically aligned, the little once spoke to him in turn in soft gentle sound combinations, "Oh, round one, fret not the loss of your life and that of this. The Igoilenat race and yours will be ours."

Eight

The off watches of the night were spent with the creatures of the hive and Oteph grew to love the life-giving aura that pervaded the galley as new kweegons were hatched almost every day. Often, he just sat in a chair and marveled at the process of a new life being created from what he saw as nothing. Life seemed to engender itself as he watched. Sure, there was the odd occasion when the hive needed protein for food, but the marvel of the hive was its never ending fecundity. Oteph learn to respect and enjoy the fellowship of the other kweegons aboard the ship. Thaulab soon took him under his wise confidence and set out to teach Oteph the ways of the mind readers.

"It's easy once you think of it," he would say to Oteph's amazement. In time Oteph learned the basics of the kweegon lifestyle and learned to control his feelings of uncontrollable rage. Oteph began to consider a life that was not possible before. Thaulab often sat beside him while watched the hive and Tovalu and the others piloted the Regiceld deeper into the territory of the Igoilenat.

"What do you think of them, Oteph," Thaulab asked with a gleam in his eye.

"I think they're marvelous. Toiling here day after day without a friend or cultivator near."

"Soon you will know that freedom, my friend."

Oteph looked at his new master and then turned back to the hive as it repeated its soft methodical vibration over and over again.

So this was life. Oteph had not known life since he had left his home on Saurus. There the sun beat down on every inch of soil and only cooled when it was invisible for the brief periods of night. All that and Saurian life and culture depended on the reclamation of the wastelands overgrown with gnarled woods and choking vines. But the hive was different. Here, life made itself anew every time he look upon its pulsating orbs. Newborn kweegons were simply the embodiment of health and fecundity. Oteph marveled, but Thaulab simply looked on with pride and satisfaction. Oteph felt his energy and it was profoundly blessed.

Nine

With each passing day, the kweegons grew more attached and amused with their prisoner. Oteph, however, needed twice the amount of food as usual to keep up his laborious studies of the former crew of the Mon Ami. Patricia I and her whilom first mate, Rafael, had modified the electrical controls of the ship in anticipation of an attack by the Visitors. If not for his outright hatred of what he called electronic meddlers, he would have had to admit their genius.

The ship's navigation program, the Radinon 2.0.0.1 was a modification that allowed minimal psi-shielding in certain decks and parts of the computer. Patricia I modified the code to include remote airlock control for the prevention of pirate raids (Oteph sniffed at the idea), cosmic billowing and vagrant particle rays. In short, Radinon-Patricia functioned closer to the fashion of a human brain than had all low-tech low-budget computers of its time. The one called Patsy knew of the dangers of the Outer and the vulnerability of her own race. Oteph grew stronger as he perused millions of lines of code simply to learn the process of automatic laundry indicators, a system that had also been subjected to redesign and "Innovations." Patricia I's addition's to the system's code was simply the complete and total linkage of every single ship function to a single dashboard. "long-winded determination of the vital versus the mundane in the ship's life. The difference was huge. Instead of a defenseless scientific scout vessel, the Mon Ami was a travelling center of protected life.

In spite of his growing knowledge of the kweegon method of life, Oteph was still muted from the loss of his tongue. Depression set in as he slowly thought about the possibility of a life without riches. "life without weapons. The Kweegons, after all, didn't value objects, just the minds and souls of the things that inhabited them. The Raison d'être of kweegon life was the body politic just as it was the action of feeding on the thoughts of others.

"We are legion," a smiling Thaulab would often say to his new apprentice. The system eventually made sense to him. The Kweegons needed the Mon Ami in order to complete a mass consumption of the Igoilenat race and the system called by them, Home.

Soon he learned to communicate through signs and psychic projections. Thaulab and his others aided the addled pirated by supporting him through vast amounts of food, mental comfort and tight physical constraint. Oteph became used to being held to a chair while his mouth and head were immobilized. He was finally ready to investigate the vanilla version of Radinon, the version most common to the Andilaxian fleet operated by the Home worlders. From start to finish, Radinon was a standard interface to modify ship's temp, oxygen that was vital to the Igoilenat species and the rudimentary control of weapons, instruments and scientific explorations. Radinon was designed to go online just seconds before live beings entered the ship and maintain them through missions of up to one hundred years. After that, the computer would be expected to fail and the life forms with it. Large cruisers carried different coding that could perform different functions but never longer than a short hundred year period and never on a mere Andilaxian craft.

Long ago, engineers of the Andilax created short and long-range battle, survey and leisure craft. The computers that had long protected their creators had no need of change and thus coding remained unchanged for several millennia. By the time the Igoilenat reached space, Saurians, like

Oteph had long since developed and used craft with larger, faster power plants, more complex quintillian shielding systems and the neutron drive equation. Piracy was an art and those like Oteph were its aficionados. The primitive Saurians were gifted and powerful rulers of the space lanes, but the Andilaxian race soon developed highly secured vessels protected by the Radinon, a computerized environmental parsing system. I due time, the need for battle-ready and robust ship's operations became realized. Thus the name Radinon. Radinon Ng was the god of skies and fires, the creator of Andilaxus and its source of the creative. Radinon the computer was capable of both military and scientific application. "leisure edition operated on some yachts and controlled pleasure nodes and deck temperatures.

Rudimentary systems like the 0.9 line were installed on freighters and small barges. In time, Radinon developed into much more than a computer. When properly configured, Radinon equipped ships wore a stronger armor than any combat vessel known to the galaxy. They were the bane of Saurian and piratical livelihood. Until the time of the seconds, the Radinons soon fell victim to telepathic attacks by such psychic species.

The Mon Ami and the Salvulent continued on a direct course through Andilaxian space as Oteph and the crew studied the most basic of the Radinon computer structures. As it happened, upon finding or being approached by a star ship outfitted with such a computer, The now studied computer director, Oteph would use a stock elude mechanism, the only one available on such an old ship. For their part, the Kweegons pooled their minds into defensive shields about the two docked ships. For days, Oteph gazed at the monitors until his eyes became sore.

"You must learn vigilance," Thaulab reminded him, "we are very close to danger. Very close."

"But if the Igoilenat attack we not only have this ship but also mine for the defense."

" My children have been playing with your toys and they won't be enough to fight against a superior craft of the modern Andilaxian Navy. I have fit your ship with new shielding and given an upgrade to the computer that should protect against computers up to the version 3."

"Excellent," Oteph laughed, "So you see, we'll just get in and get out and maybe take a few things as well. I heard that the Recipro have the highest tech numbers of any modern fleet outside of the Ng superstation."

Thaulab turned away from him and looked at a monitor on the vertical dashboard. Two ships approached. One of them was large like a sailing yacht and the other was small like an escort fighter. Together, they meant trouble. Thaulab rushed out of the bridge area and down the corridor to the galley where eighty of his kind sat and played relaxing games of cards and mental blocking.

"Pierre, Korg, Tuvalo. Come." At once three large beings rose from their chairs and followed Thaulab from the room. Although they bore many of the same features, the three Kweegons were decidedly different in aspect and facial appearance. Pierre, the tallest of the bunch, wore a short white beard that curled around his neck and nearly covered his snout. Korg, the shortest and fattest, wore spectacles always carried a bag of food with him. His body was nearly free of hair and his face was light green with large pink splotches. His tentacled fingers were also covered by a pink skin that indicated more of a disease than a racial characteristic. Strangely enough, they all came from the same planet

Tuvalo was tall, muscular and always sneered at those he met in corridors, along streets and in nearly every place that people met. His mannerisms were strange for a person who truly loved others and always looked for the best in those he met. Those who knew him, loved him and those who didn't were terrified to look at him.

"You're a pleasant book with a nasty cover," Thaulab used to chide. Tuvalo didn't care. It was up to him to save his dying race from the ever-expanding population of hominids that polluted the space that once belonged to his ancestors.

Oteph was a strange friend among such people. Being a hominid, he was hated, but being hated by other hominids made him a powerful ally. The Kweegons depended on him to guide system attacks against enemy computers. Only he knew how the Igoilenat configured their environmental controls. With his help, Thaulab and his family had successfully hijacked three older fighters and a cargo barge. Oteph was a quick study when it came to stealing things. Thaulab loved to see his hungry, lusty smile appear whenever the Andilaxian craft came into range.

"You want me go get 'em?" He would ask in his garbled, tongue-less speech. Thaulab would laugh within his mind at such things. We'll go far with this guy, he thought.

Thaulab stood vigilantly on the bridge with his three main officers and viewed that data screens that indicated the approach of the cruiser and its escort. Tuvalo held his fingers to his head as if to launch an attack on the ship.

"Belay that, Val," Thaulab said, "Let's invite them in. Oteph. Detach the barge."

Oteph did as he was told and watched as the large massive object began hurtling toward the cruiser that now seemed dwarfed by the size of the massive barge. "t first, the cruiser began to spin in an identical course away from the barge. Oteph quickly took control of the barge by running its physical plant through Mon Ami's Radinon. The cruiser shot rounds of reflective chaff to disorient the drive systems of the large ship, but when this didn't work, the barge was pelted by laser cannons from the cruiser. Finally, a slow flying torpedo finished off what was left of the barge.

"Let me at em, Thaulab," Oteph mumbled, "They can't dodge the Salvulent like that."

"Indeed they cannot, young pirate. And yet you cannot dodge them."

The Mon-Ami continued its slow course into the Andilaxian region stopping only to recalibrate instruments thrown off by the accidental approach of the nearby Ng system.

The attacks came quickly. Out of nowhere, tiny cruisers surrounded the conglomeration of ships. Tuvalo was dispatched immediately to the Salvulent while Oteph and others of the kweegon crew operated the two smaller cruisers. Thaulab stayed behind in the Mon Ami to direct its movements and perhaps gain an edge over the leaner, smarter ships of the Ng empire. Even with Patricia I's creative developments to the Radinon 2, the Mon Ami lay naked against highly effective computer attacks while kweegon pilots and Oteph himself sought to draw fire away from their flagship, the broken-down survey ship. For hours, skillful piloting and creative thinking led the Ng corsairs away from the battle, but the success was short because the much newer ships bore complete psychic shielding and unbreakable computer systems. Thaulab pounded his flat hand against the dashboard as he saw his two ancient cruisers succumb to the superior abilities of the small defensive fleet of the Ng system. Of his two old cruisers, only one made it back to Mon Ami. Bleeding and clearly fatigued, Oteph blustered through the airlock slamming his large clumsy feet against either side of the walkway.

"They're too fast. Too many of 'em."

Ten

The fighters and cruisers had disappeared momentarily as if to indicate a victory for the small force of kweegons and their impromptu fleet of two elderly cruisers and a disabled barge. Soon, however, the Ng system defense boats returned and compelled the captain to comply with a mandatory course to Our, the central gas giant of the system. Our was a water-covered world surrounded by three moons and an asteroid belt. As Oteph sat trembling in his captain's chair. The Mon Ami was pulled into space dock where soldiers waited to escort them to a prison boat. In the next few hours, the crew of the Mon Ami were denied food and stood in the cold storage facility, the kweegons grew pale and gradually started to collapse upon themselves.

To a kweegons a highly humid atmosphere is just as necessary as sweltering hot conditions are to the lives of cold-blooded reptiles. Thaulab reclined in a corner while joints slowly froze and his many tentacled hands clenched together against the cold. Oteph, more accustomed to cold conditions stood by the door and continually attempted to break the lock. Oteph's fellow captives looked with interest at what the fat man was doing and at each failure to crack a certain combination, they each breathed a sigh of worry.

"Will we never get out," voiced Thaulab. Tovalu sat in the corner nursing his bloodied shoulder, but he looked longingly towards Oteph as the question was answered.

"No. The answer is 'not soon" Have to crack the basic chamber lock to release the locking mechanism of the combination key." Thaulab's mouth hung open as he tried to understand what the tall humanoid was trying to say.

"Better to just stay put. Oteph relax yourself. Wait for an opportunity."

The opportunity came after what seemed like ages in the damp dank prison cell. By this time most of the kweegons had become sick, tired or ill and, in some cases, all three from the lack of moisture in the air. Oteph lay in deep meditation by the when a guard of Ng strode in and flipped pieces of flat bread on the ground for the kweegons to pick up and eat. Rising with lightning-quick reflexes. Oteph sprang upon the guard. Oteph's large size and thick coating of fat provided enough force and inertia to slam the guard to the floor and then take his key card which was, regrettably only useful in citadel chambers. Since the door remained open, however, the kweegons slowly rose to their feet and followed their newfound hero.

"You've done it this time, fat one," Thaulab said with a grin.

The small party of kweegons included Tovalu, Pierre, Bo'agg, Thaulab and Ceati. As they forced themselves into upright positions, they managed to take a few steps out into the corridor before collapsing in fatigue. The cold had been more destructive than even Oteph had thought. Not everything held the sheer lard percentage as a massive space whale. Oteph looked with pity and even great concern over his new brothers. Would they die without him? Did he kill them? Such thoughts of guilt circled like so many tempests in his primitive but caring mind.

It was no short time after the kweegons lay down than they began to feel the warmth of the complex that were able to stand again. Tovalu stretched his massive frame upwards towards the ceiling wile Pierre and Bo'agg rose more slowly as if from a deep, drug-induced trance. Thaulab, himself, had no intention of waiting another instant in the dangerous area and jumped to his feet lifting Ceati by the carapace and setting him upright again.

"We have much to lose by this slowness," he grumbled, "get up and get out!"

The code of companions followed his advice and darted to the nearest hiding place, a small communications booth.

Eleven

"Two of them," he said, " laser carbines. "Tovalu, get ready. The rest of you, hide and concentrate." The remaining Kweegons did as they were told and hid behind the still open door of the cell. The two guards made their way slowly to the corridor where Tovalu lay in wait for them.

"Now," Tovalu cried. The meditating Kweegons conjured an astral projection of a large beast that walked on four knurled and calloused legs. On its feet were short, timeworn claws.

"Yeah, right," Tovalu said, but the deed worked and the projected creature became real and palpable to the approaching villains. In the presence of the mighty beast, they shrunk away in horror

The two guards wearing reflective tunics bore power packs and laser rifles which they immediately employed on the large hairy creature. The creature howled in pain shuddering with each new blast of concentrated radiation. It was not long until the guards realized they were fighting against a figment of their imagination. The massive creature vanished as a cloud and they were left looking straight in the face of the Saurian pirate that had helped their escape. With a flick of his mighty wrist, Oteph used his electro-flag to dash the laser rifles to pieces even as they were in the hands of their owners. Slowly but confidently, the Kweegons gathered underneath the big man's massive shadow. Separately, they were unable to fight off the guards but with the help of Oteph and his mighty arms, they concentrated and watched as the two guards ran away as children do when they are released from the discipline of a holding block.

"Now. What next?"

"We have no shuttle. The Mon Ami is gone forever," Tovalu said dejectedly.

"No," said Thaulab in a more optimistic tone, "We must start again. Get out of this system and head for Home world, but there are many things to do here and now." Thaulab made a light dramatic sweep of his right arm as if to bring importance to the things he said.

"Well. We'll steal one of theirs". Perhaps a powerful friend and a Radinon class three computer."

" You know we can't do that, Tom. Andilax has been fitting their ships with the mark fours for several years now.

"Correction," Thaulab replied," Only on their best warships are these computers installed. Besides we have the knowledge of Patricia I buried deep inside that vacuous hole between your ears."

"I resent that. Especially coming from a walking bogey of a man."

"We must get started," Pierre said as he quietly rose from his hiding place in the cell. He watched his elders grumbling over the niceties or lack thereof of invading the capitol city. The sought a spacecraft with a significant tech level that would take them to a safe location near Home world, the home of the hated Igoilenat peoples. The small band of adventurers walked in near lock step as they undulated down the corridors. Tentacled hands and feet made it easy to cling and swing from the walls and ceiling while Oteph huffed and puffed as he dragged his fat body across the floor. The situation would have been humorous if not for the impending violence that was about to befall the owner of the large clanking boot soles.

The Mon Ami had its adhesive powder, other ships had electrified flooring, but the corridor surfaces of the Ng central command station possessed reverberating hummers.

The hummers sent activity data to a central computer that deployed scouts and police to investigate and eliminate possible threats to the stations safety. Thus, as Oteph stepped quietly down the hallway, flag in hand, he had no idea that his softly moving feet were being recorded far away in the command tower and that yet another patrol was headed their way. But he did not worry. Instead, he stared blankly at his companions that sat shivering against the cold on a strange floor in a strange part of a planet they knew nothing about.

Oteph looked at them with a measure of pity. How interesting that such mighty creatures could be brought to nothing by the simple change in climate that new surroundings afford. Thaulab and Tovalu were the first to rise while Pierre and Bo'agg followed close behind. Security camera were present at nearly every corner of the complex. Oteph decided it was high time for him to use his new knowledge of computers to manipulate the cameras so that they showed images of their source rather than giving away his position.

The security command center was apparently located on level four, b-wing seventy-seven.

"Hey Val," he called, "take a look at this. Just a swarm

"You're right, fat one, there's little time, and we must get those guns."

Thaulab looked longingly at the scene on the monitor that showed a window that looked out on verdant pastures and a vast sea in the distance. "t each security station, the party looked upwards to monitor the presence of hostile guards and to find more information about the layout of the center. After hours of deliberated searching, the guard house was finally in view. Picking up weapons was easy, but fitting them to each differently shaped Kweegon was difficult. Tovalu naturally request a large missile launcher, while Pierre and Bo'agg preferred simple laser pistols that they could hide in their breeches. "t long last, they were ready to move on . Oteph grabbed a portable scanner that would serve them as a navigational aid. The technology and science decks were located on floor three, but the main air-dock was located on nine deck, the tallest of the suspended surfaces.

Oteph seemed peaceful as he took up a position behind some rubbish. Fingering the tip of his whip, he sneered with what seemed to be pure greed at a fully loaded merchant ship that sat just on the opposite side of the deck being unloaded by a crew of dock workers. He glanced knowingly at the small band of Kweegons that he considered his friends. Thaulab bowed his head very slightly and placed his hand on the small laser pistol he had borrowed from the security locker.

Bo'agg and Pierre did the same while Tovalu took up a position that would allow a straight shot towards the service deck should the little pirates be seen. As fat and as clumsy as he was, Oteph could move silently as a feather when he needed to. On this occasion, he crept silently up the side of the launch pad. He drew within ten yards of the craft and then signaled for the rest of the party to follow.

The merchant ship was practically brand-new. It was of Andilaxian origin and, by its paint, belonged to the Inner Home system mercantile marine. The small ramp extended from the lower part of the storage bay to the floor where the workers were clearing cargo. It was not long before Oteph was noticed by security police that looked down upon the cargo shuttles and the men who worked there. Sirens flashed with purple and red lights while workers dropped their carts boxes and data tablets. Oteph rushed toward the ship waving to his companions to follow him. If he ever got the bird out of the dock he would be very happy. Unfortunately, he had no experience with the third-generation of Andilaxian ships.

The craftsmen of the Andilax system, had completed a set of controls that were uniquely suited for those of Igoilenat ancestry. But the Igoilenat were a hideous race with three-fingered paws, slobbery mouths and long, rat-like tails.

Oteph poured over the unfamiliar buttons of the main dashboard. So much had changed since the time of the Mon Ami and its primitive construction, that buttons had been redefined, scanner screens made into interactive holographic images. Luckily, it only took Thaulab and Tovalu the better part of thirty seconds to decipher the controls and set the ship on an escape route away from the docking station on Ng beta. The ploy worked in no small thanks to abilities of the Kweegons. Tovalu grasped the armrests of his command chair.

"I think we did it. Now to get past the guards." Tovalu frowned at he looked out at the ever-diminishing planet and then towards each horizon where there lay ten battle satellites ready to send them hurtling back to close orbital reach of the planet's air and defense force. Tovalu learned to use the guns of Andilaxian craft and these were no different. While he lay reflective chaff out of rear turrets, he trained the small merchant's missile turret toward one of the satellites. Within moments of impact, the small space weapon flashed momentarily and then was doused like candle pinched between two fingers. It was not long until Tovalu grew accustomed to the weapons console and, indeed, derived much pleasure in the pursuit.

Oteph sat dejectedly at the dashboard while he watched his fellows interact with the ship's computer creating a myriad of new defensive and offensive maneuvers every second that they were in view of a satellite. This was no Survey shuttle. This was a space craft. Oteph longed for the days when crashing down doors and slashing enemies in the face with his whip were the goal of the day. Oteph reason for being was now tied up in the future of these three little aliens. Every day he became less a Saurian and more a growing convert to the psychic determinism of the Kweegons. So they set out among the stars, not considering how far the tiny merchant would take them or if they had a chance of conquering the hated Igoilenat.

The Regiceld, for so it was called, was equipped with a slower than light propulsion unit that allowed the craft to travel up to half distances between a system's core or between a system and halfway to the next. Previous pilots of the ship had affectionately termed it the "Halvsy", but their undying devotion to the Regiceld was solid. The Regiceld was heavily armored for its size, completely shielded against psychic attack and the use of astral projections. Its kweegon pilots, however meant to reprogram the shielding units to reflect amplified psychic force fields toward enemies and to cause catastrophic system failure in approaching hostile ships. The idea was ingenious and Pierre smiled for weeks after he had come up with the thought. It took weeks of hard , sweaty work until Oteph was able to rewire the ship's defensive shielding system. During this time, the ship lay vulnerable to even the smallest passing dust particle. Thus, Bo'agg and his elder brother Tovalu formed a canopy across all parts of the ships exposed hull. It wasn't much, but it protected the ship while repairs were being made. A stolen ship is no welcome guest at a star port.

Once the Regiceld was repaired, modified and otherwise improved, it was time to move into a regular schedule of upkeep and embarking on the journey to the Home planet of the Igoilenat. Comforted by the success of his repair job, Oteph began to eat more and gained weight. Unfortunately, the galley served a double role as a cargo hold and was, at the time, completely filled with boxes of metal ore. He observed how a pull-away section in the wall could be utilized as a ramp. He went away dejectedly and more hungry than ever.

Weeks passed as the merchant ship lumbered out of the Ng system and into deep space. Here in the world between the worlds, Oteph and his crew could see the wisdom of the universe. Four corners came together at this one juncture, the Igoilenat main system of Home. The Andilaxian, Saurian and Xerxian peoples all came to this place as common ground. It was a place of paradise for space pirates. Oteph smiled at the prospect of some thievery or at least some dancing about where money and life hangs in the balance.

"Can't we stay? We need better stuff than this," he said while waving a hand at the computerized weapons console.

"True. We do need that, but, most of all, we need you," Tovalu said in a deep growling voice, "We need you as our pilot."

Oteph understood what he meant, but stealing was his bag Direct confrontation with naval ships of one of the great civilizations of the realm didn't impress him.

"We're running low on fuel. We need to stop," Oteph answered, "Once we drop this shipment, we can find another more important cargo." Oteph grinned through his yellow-stained teeth.

"Anyway, right here. That's where we'll go, Org delta one. It's a moon. They have a port, women, booze and guns: the works." So the intrepid and unafraid crew directed themselves to the tiny planetary system that lay just out of Igoilenat space.

Oteph commanded the Regiceld with the ease and aplomb of an experienced spacer. After all, he was no novice in the operation of space equipment. He quickly grew accustomed to the controls and the computer and trained his kweegon cohorts to fall in behind him as successful crew members. As the ships slowly approached Org Delta One, intercepting spacecraft rushed out to meet them.

Identify origin and purpose," a computer-simulated voice intoned across the comlink. Oteph waved his hand toward the crew and silently programmed a bio-intendor into the Radinon.

"It's highly unlikely, but I think I can squelch their main operating system," Oteph finally said as beads of sweat started to gather on his forehead.

"Code Error" The ship's computer answered, "You are using a Radinon 2 to squelch a Polik 20. State origin and purpose." Oteph was losing his cool handed attitude. Looking back at Thaulab, he silently pleaded for an answer to the problem

"Very well, large one, this looks like a job an old kweegon can solve. Brothers, join me." Tovalu, Pierre and Bo'agg centered their tentacled hands over the console of the Radinon. Soon, a screeching sound arose and the entire computer station . Soon, the control room seemed to fill itself with unrelenting heat. The buzzing of the console became a whirring inside Oteph's head. Oteph felt as though his head would explode starting with his Eustachian tubes and ending with the most complex centers of his brain. To reassure himself, he placed his hands over his ears, but there seemed to be no escape from the noise.

"Oteph, get out of here," he heard Thaulab's voice sounding in his mind, "We are about to create the derelict." Oteph knew what that meant. The kweegon crew of the Regiceld were about to capture an entire spacecraft, place its crew into deep hibernation and take over the ship's intelligent resources, in this case the Polik. Oteph took Thaulab's advice and ran down the corridor from the bridge, but he only just arrived at the mid ship's air lock when the mental offensive reached its peak. He felt himself flying and then slipping into a dark place. Oteph awoke some days later to see Thaulab and the crew bending over and peering at him as though he were a piece of rotten fruit.

"Yes," he began, "very difficult for the mentally simple to withstand a basic attack." Oteph attempted to rise from the bed and argue the point, but he felt as though he were paralyzed: literally transfixed to the seemingly heavy paper blanket and small medical towel that held his head in a more comfortable position. "No, do not rise. You are not free of your sickness. Next time, you'll wear the psi-cloak."

Days of recovery seemed to be like weeks for Oteph and when he finally awoke, he realized that, like any other member of his species, lack of consciousness meant lack of biological enhancement, nourishment and muscle control. When he awoke, he brought his legs from between the sheets to a place where they sat evenly on the floor. As he made an effort to stand, his legs buckled beneath and he slumped to the ground. As he lay helplessly on the floor, Oteph looked up at the ceiling and noted how far away it seemed to have become. Eventually, as he rose slowly to his feet, he made his way to the galley where he felt that he owed himself a month's worth of food. By dead reckoning, the crossing of the nexus took one month of small, deliberate tacking that led the Regiceld into range of the Home system. Once there, Oteph resumed his post at the captain's chair while Thaulab, Tovalu and Pierre cycled through duties at the computer, scanners and navigational consoles. The wreck of the system defense cruiser spun aimlessly about the high outer orbit of Org delta one and became a subject of conversation among the crew. Oteph, himself, looked out the port holes at the derelict craft with a wonder that reminded him of his earliest days of space faring. The shining visage of a craft that was ripe with supplies, ammunition and weapons. Oteph remembered the days of old when he used to dream of other, greater ships than the Salvulent B. The defense cruiser would have suited him just fine, but Thaulab and his crew were unfazed by its presence, operating or not, and strangely unperturbed by the lack of feeling toward the derelict's crew who would now, like Patricia and Rafael, live on in perpetual paralyzed sleep. The thoughts bothered Oteph, but he stowed them away in his heart. He no longer traveled with his own kind and he began to trust Thaulab implicitly in all shipboard decisions. The kweegons, strange as they were, became his platonic comrades and fellows. Binding the defense boat to the larger flotilla took weeks until a suitable pilot and computer operator were found among the young of the hive. Truly, Oteph and Thaulab commanded a formidable naval force capable of terrible deeds.

Traversing the Nexus was no easy feat and the process, done safely, entailed months of minuscule maneuvers finally brought the Regiceld into the range of normal navigation to the next star system. Oteph sat on the bridge and frowned at the readouts and blips that lit up the main console. By this time, the Andilaxian ships were becoming more common just as the incidence of the Xerxian and Saurian ships started to dwindle. "t last, the Regiceld needed more fuel and got some on the asteroid, Mdukai. Oteph walked about the dusty ground and looked skyward to his home world , Saurus three. He felt a wave of guilt rush over him. After the conquest of Home, the Kweegons intended to turn their eyes and tentacles toward Saurus and the Saurian civilization. It would be the last he ever saw of the culture that raised him, tortured him and otherwise drew him to the stars and a life of pirating. First things first, Tovalu nervously guided his tentacles over the controls of the dashboard. The Regiceld had been hailed by an observer.

"Hail, Regula Regiceld, state your numbers and your purpose." Tovalu remained silent at the console and broadcast over the communicator. "Regula Regiceld. Hey, answer guys! You've got no business here if you can't talk." Once again, Tovalu remained in deep contemplation and filled the lines with perfect static. "Regula, you must respond or be attacked and forced to land." "t this point, Tovalu knew what he would do. He spun the ship around until its hard points were trained on the source of the security transmission. Oteph took the signal from Thaulab and rushed down the corridor to the docking bay. In moments, the ship's boat appeared from beneath the main hull and the heavily armored and armed ship started to pelt the security station with tight surgical blasts. With one final missile drop, the station was obliterated with only a billowing structural frame left behind.

"Get out of there!" Tovalu screamed at Oteph in the boat. Oteph had swung forward to see the damage in detail and to perhaps reconnoiter the possibilities of an impromptu base or redoubt. After all, fighting the Igoilenat is something that many had tried and failed at and life would only become harder the closer they drew to Home and the environs of the human-led armies. But their approach was also noted by the Igoilenat.

As the team aboard the Regiceld approached Home, they intercepted news and political broadcasts. Everywhere, nations panicked at the psychic forecast that predicted the coming of Visitors to Home. Children and adults fumbled with psi-shielding helmets, called brain boxes by the elite who did not think they needed them

The hysteria over Visitors did not limit itself to Home planet proper, but rumors and fear spread to the six moons and asteroid communities in the outlands. But hysteria also spread to the presidential council of military endeavors. New weapons were rolled out immediately. Since hi-tech weapons had proved useless against telepathic creatures in the past. Home gathered together the most ancient of its conventional warring squadron. thousands of bombers, localized nuclear bombs weather controlling devices all brought together the sum of Home's defenses. The sight of all the pitiable and ancient weapons caused the people to weep for their own despair and the death of their race.

Home was governed by two thousand local tyrants, three of which were absolute. In the time of the Visitor's attack, the tyrants glued themselves together to form armies that would save their common assets and insure a familiar future for all parties involved.

Oteph slopped himself across a cabin chair as he watched the scanners as they fed data into the Radinon 2 about Home, its atmospheric content, it sustain ability for life and its habitability for oxygen breathing organisms

"Well," he said indicating the scanner, "Whatever's down there, we're sure gonna kill the Hell out of it."

"Study it," hummed Tovalu.

"OK. Study it, then we kill it"

"I don't know why we don't just go and tie you up again."

Oteph glanced at the screen and silently thought to himself. Tovalu who sat behind the navigation console made frequent use of the computer to adjust the ability of the ship to use psychic warfare. The Regiceld now had the capability of projecting small ships, scows and fighters in medium to long range distance from attacking ships. Just like Oteph was proud to have repaired the psi-shielding, Tovalu was proud of his equally important work on the computer. He felt every bit the genius that Patricia I must have been when she modified a mark 2 ship's computer into that which would equal the power of a mark 3. Tovalu, on the other hand, started with the Mark 3 computer but he was able to modify it to the standards of the common Mark V versions that were so common nowadays.

Home system was different from most systems of charted space. It was at the exact nexus of all five great races and it was also home to many of the most habitable planets in any one system in any region of space. Home was the living space of many different races from the rat like Igoilenat to the horse-like hounyms that lived on Home beta seven. " Myriad of oceanic life teemed within the seas of Home and "darastra. Frozen methane coated many lifeless asteroids, but the flying boulders were still home to some of the most valuable mineral veins in the galaxy. Interstellar trade was well developed within the realm of the Home system and it was easy to see why scientific studies of the Outland were so odd and interesting. In fact, it was the interstellar trader that created the stir in high society of Igoilenat culture. The approach of a merchant ship was always the source of much excitement and intrigue that citizens gazed heavenward whenever they had a chance to. However, the Regiceld was no welcome guest. As soon as the word came around that it was a visitor ship, Home's outer defenses were sealed and intercepting warships were dispatched. As with the Mon Ami, fully outfitted system ships were no match for the enhanced Regiceld that darted, dashed, listed and warped all the while picking apart the opposition with the clever piloting of Oteph, the sheer concentration of the lesser Kweegons and the mad navigational techniques of Tovalu. Within moment of the Igoilenat attack, the space lanes were quiet again, and the crew of the Regiceld looked toward Home, their destination in a week or more. It was at such times that Thaulab and the children would huddle closely in the bridge and communicate with Radinon, plotting a more perfect courses

***

With Home's defenses all but gone and planet wide hysteria already set well in, The crew of Regiceld, the Visitors, slowly approached the impending doom of yet another civilization. The constant hum of the thrust drive and the whirring of the oxygen ports made for a certain amount of pre-invasion atmosphere. Thaulab leaned back in his captain's chair and folded his hands together. Home was still seven day away , but it already appeared as a bright gem against the deep black of space.

Deep space allowed for certain absolutes and these were, the speed of the half-drive, the speed of light through the dark recesses of space and the certainty of habitable worlds. Home and Ng were companion stars. revolving around each other, planets of one system often dipped into the realm of the other. Ng bet seven often drifted toward Home whereas Home delta one was so small and so far from Home's core, that it actually became part of the Ng system on a regular basis.

The rotations of the two suns were a mystery to Oteph, but his crew mates took the discrepancies in stride It was there that the Regiceld found itself, lacking fuel, oxygen and food. And yet again, they had to leave empty with dirty duel in the tanks, decayed food in the galley and more than a little recycled water.

Once again, it was time to run. with only a half supply of refined fuel, they would have to go out of system to collect the things they needed. The plan was made to go into Xerxian space, a neighboring world on the edge of the kweegon realm. Oteph looked at the dash with wonder as he tried to decipher the movement of the planets. Looking at the universe from the smallest planet in the

Ng/Home system was more difficult than it looked. Oteph had learned to manage the controls of the small freighter, but he was unsure of most of the powerful functions thereof. He came to trust in and befriend Tovalu. It wasn't easy for him to need a friend, because he lived so long as a hated parasitic creature since the time that he stole the Salvulent. As Oteph sat motionless at the dash, he secretly eyed Tovalu. He'd never had a friend, at least not long enough to express his own faithfulness.

Oteph viewed Thaulab, Pierre, Bo'agg and Tovalu as his friends. After years of hating everybody, not knowing anybody and neither wanting to know. It was going to be hard, but Oteph knew he had found a place in life after all. Thaulab seemed to approve of his constant progress in the area of mind control and an ever deepening of his knowledge of the ship's systems. Soon, he was creating new algorithms for Radinon Four, plotting courses within and without Ng and was finally beginning to accurately track the Igoilenat trade routes and how they operated. However, attacking Home was no longer an option. Floating like a tiny cork on top of a basin of water, The Regiceld was not properly outfitted for corsair duties, but with Oteph the captain, the hijacking of trade returned to normal. Oteph us was happy,

Thaulab was thoughtful and Tovalu and the rest were guardedly optimistic.

Within two months, The Visitors had captured three fighters, forty decatons of cargo and stymied the Ng navy as many times as they tried. If it was important for the Kweegons to capture and assemble an army of their own, it was equally imperative that trade be done with other pirate communities. The Regiceld, was, after all, a merchant and not a corsair as were some of the newly hijacked vessels. The Kweegons traveled in a rotating formation to prevent the possibility of attack by legitimate traders and warships.

In these days of closeness to Andilaxian space, Oteph left the console for meals and to relieve himself. The former, he managed to sneak on the bridge so he had something to munch on during the long hours of planning an entry into the Home system. They stayed in a holding pattern for months that seemed like years and eventually fell prey to people of their own ilk.

"bout six months from their internment at Ng, fleeing from system police, Oteph and the flotilla remained motionless in a turbulent crosswind of gravitational fields. They were powerless against the laws of space and nature and when he was about to give up, Oteph looked to Tovalu for some encouragement.

Just keep it steady," he said, "I think I've got a fix."

This was good news, at least, because Oteph noticed the approach of five tiny specks on the down-looking dashboard. They had been found. Well, here we go again, he grunted. Placing the ship's systems on hold, he sprung from his seat and sped down the corridor to the communication shaft. Here, Tovalu, Bo'agg, Pierre and Thaulab stood waiting for him.

"Your word?"

"Battle stations," he said, barely looking up from the floor. Tovalu's lithe body shot through the hatch and was followed by the shorter Pierre and Bo'agg. Thaulab took his time entering the shaft. He seemed to be physically weak from some sort of malady. Whatever it was and whenever it happened, Oteph didn't care. Soon the flotilla of ships was activated and began to swarm around the approaching fighters.

When attacking hostiles, Oteph had learned the combat trade secrets of the Kweegons. Flying in a loose diamond configuration, the Kweegons were better able to project false images and intimidate the attackers into thinking they were attacking a massive navy when they were, in fact, fighting an old merchant ship, two fighters and a cargo scow. astral projection of the barge transformed it into a corsair with heavy armament and ability to out maneuver any small attack ship in the galaxy. The truth was, however, that the scow had only one defensive sand caster and an even smaller laser cannon. It was well-suited to its purpose, but it was not suited for battle. Thaulab and his men remained in a secondary triangle behind Oteph and Tovalu. It was there that they, the barge and the younger Kweegons set about to attack the computers of the oncoming ships. This was the most familiar type of warfare that Kweegons ever practiced. Once inside a computer, they could absorb all of the ship's data, navigational settings and targeting projections. Thus, it was a frolicsome pass time to watch the humanoid pilots try to shoot each other in the sky. The only problem was with the damaged equipment that had to be disposed of after the battle. Kweegons were smart, but they always left some kind of trail of wrecked ships, hollowed out space ports.

"t the end of the battle, the barge had taken the hardest hits of all leaving it listing precariously far from the Regiceld that had been ambling forward at a snail's pace while the battle raged.

"Where the hell were you guys?" Oteph yelled as he saw Pierre, Bo'agg and Tovalu entering the ship, "Can't I get any support? Just for once? Huh!" Oteph's face was red with anger.

"Your problem is...your anger O fat one," a relaxed Thaulab said. Pierre and Bo'agg stayed around long enough to blow their snouts at him and then departed to the galley where the rest of the "family" was growing.

"We had to stay back. It's customary."

"Customary to leave me among those savages," Oteph snorted.

"Clearly you haven't learned," Thaulab said quietly and mournfully, "Perhaps we cannot teach you."

Thaulab' soft voice always burned Oteph. Generally always correct, he had said the truth this time. He must learn to control his anger, concentrate on the good of the Kweegons race and to let go of who he was as an individual, obstreperous, self-involved pirate. To him, the thought of it was crushing and to perform that which was needed was even more foreign to him. Oteph looked at his boots and shuffled down to the galley where he met the youngest of the Kweegons. They were easier to be around. They didn't judge, they didn't correct and they certainly couldn't discern him from any other person aboard. Oteph was only at home in a cloud of lies and with the younger ones, he could be whoever he wanted to be.

Reaching an escape vector into the Home system took quite some time, but eventually the flotilla managed to safely drift into the neighboring system without fear of being drawn back to Ng.

Home system differed much from that of Ng in that three of its planets were more or less habitable. Of those, two, Gocuda and Heewheg were water worlds, the former an ice capped barren globe while Heewheg was a balmy, highly humid ocean world. The largest and most advanced of Home's planets was Gyukk, a planet with habitable regions, agricultural commodities, mineral deposits, food and even refined fuel. Luckily Gyukk was their next stop before heading on towards the waterworlds and the asteroid belt that ringed Home like a wide leather girdle.

"Is it time?" Oteph said as he looked at Thaulab. Getting an affirmative nod, he signaled to Tovalu that the landing process was to begin. The merchant ship had a small planetary boat, but Oteph and the crew expected trouble. Thus, the barge and two fighters were sent to the planet's surface to retrieve food and fuel and hopefully to offload some cargo from the vast holds of the Regiceld.

Gyuuk was home to some of the finest amenities known to local and deep space, thus the importance of her capture. The barge and the two fighters set down easily on a port that looked over vast roiling sea. The landing pad stood far above the surface of the planet, but supplies and trade were able to be transferred without undue interaction with the planet's normal state of affairs. It was a cargo factory. Large load-bearing robots relieved the barge of its contents while individual cart-masters inspected the fuel holds of the two fighters. Pierre and Bo'agg, two young pilots looked on as their ships were being examined, poked and prodded. As for the barge, it was quickly loaded with fuel and ready to return to low orbit about the planet. Pierre and Bo'agg could not believe that the task could have been so simple, and yet it wasn't. As soon as the barge left the pad, dock workers turned to look at them. Pierre and Bo'agg had used a false projection of themselves to hide their ideas and thus they looked like shorter-than-usual swarthy Andilaxians.

"Hey. Who are you guys?" One of the men asked. Bo'agg began to shake uncontrollably. He had never been this close to a humanoid besides Oteph who was a friend.

"We're here to barter for supplies and fuel," Bo'agg could feel his skin growing warmer by the minute. Beads of sweat began to gather on his soft hide and as his fear grew, his camouflage began to flicker and he started to appear as an alien to those on the deck.

"Wait!" he yelled "You're a visitor come to bleed us dry. The dock master was a short, sweaty young man who carried a pipe in his hand and a large metal beam in the other.

His eyes blazed with anger, "You killed my father."

Bo'agg began to panic all over again. Who was his father and why should I care, he thought. Pierre stood boldly by the side of his friend.

"We don't know your foolish talk, savage," Bo'agg answer, "We come in peace, but could depart in war."Pierre seemed to derive pleasure at making the dock masters angry. He smiled to himself.

"Bloody visitors. Just come to destroy me."

"Kweegons, actually," he said, "We just want what's ours and we'll leave you in peace...maybe."

Since the dock masters stood resolute in their defense against they whom they called visitors. Bo'agg and Pierre exchanged troubled glances.

I'm afraid they suspect. Got to get back somehow. Must tell master Tovalu.

As they silently communicated, Pierre used his affectation to train one of the ship's lasers at the deck. As soon as the ship started firing, Bo'agg and Pierre ran for cover and heaved themselves up the side of the star fighters. Within minutes, both crafts were airborne and systematically destroying the port one section at a time. When the port was no more than a burning shard of metal and composite, system defense boats seem to appear from nowhere. From low tech fighter jets to fusion caterpillar driven sky trucks, they all converged on Pierre and Bo'agg as they were caught destroying the last of the sky port. Luckily, the Ng craft was more nimble and light than were the system defense force and a relatively easy escape was possible with only a small bit of concentration. But Bo'agg wasn't the experienced pilot that Pierre was. Too many hours in recreation and the galley had left his mind soft and his belly continually larger. It was not long before the Gyuuk navy caught him in a tailwind and sent him hurtling through the atmosphere to the ocean below. It was humiliating but since he was slack in his studies as a pilot he deserved such a fate. He managed to ditch his craft before it slammed into the waves. In due time, he found himself in the water. Kweegons lived and breathed the water and it was not long until Gyuuk had been transformed almost overnight into a fertile Hive that produced scores of offspring every day.

Twelve

Two of them," he said, " laser carbines. Tovalu, get ready. The rest of you, hide and concentrate." The remaining Kweegons did as they were told and hid behind the still open door of the cell. The two guards made their way slowly to the corridor where Tovalu lay in wait for them.

"Now," Tovalu cried. The meditating Kweegons conjured an astral projection of a large beast that walked on four knurled and calloused legs. On its feet were short, timeworn claws. "Yeah, right," Tovalu said, but the deed worked and the projected creature became real and palpable to the approaching villains.

The two guards wearing reflective tunics bore power packs and laser rifles which they immediately employed on the large hairy creature. The creature howled in pain shuddering with each new blast of concentrated radiation. It was not long until the guards realized they were fighting against a figment of their imagination. The massive creature vanished as a cloud and they were left looking straight in the face of the Saurian pirate that had helped their escape. With a flick of his mighty wrist, Oteph used his electro-flag to dash the laser rifles to pieces even as they were in the hands of their owners. Slowly but confidently, the Kweegons gathered underneath the big man's massive shadow. Separately, they were unable to fight off the guards but with the help of Oteph and his mighty arms, they concentrated and watched as the two guards ran away as children do when they are released from the discipline of a holding block.

"Now. What next?"

1"We have no shuttle. The Mon Ami is gone forever," Tovalu said dejectedly.

"No," said Thaulab in a similarly depressed tone, "We must start again. Get out of this system and head for Home world, but there are many things to do here... and now." Thaulab made a light dramatic sweep of his right arm as if to bring importance to the things he said.

Like What," Oteph snorted, his fat chest rising with pride.

"Well. A ship. Perhaps a powerful friend and a Radinon class three computer."

" You know we can't do that, Tom. Andilax has been fitting their ships with the mark fours for several years now.

"Correction," Thaulab replied," Only on their best warships are these computers installed. Besides we have the knowledge of Patricia I buried deep inside that vacuous hole between your ears."

"I resent that. Especially coming from a walking sea slime."

"We must get started," Pierre said as he quietly rose from his hiding place in the cell. He watched his elders grumbling over the niceties or lack thereof of invading the capitol city. The sought a spacecraft with a significant tech level that would take them to a safe location near Home world, the home of the hated Igoilenat peoples. The small band of adventurers walked in near lock step as they undulated down the corridors. Tentacled hands and feet made it easy to cling and swing from the walls and ceiling while Oteph huffed and puffed as he dragged his fat body across the floor. The situation would have been humorous if not for the impending violence that was about to befall the owner of the large clanking boot soles.

The Mon Ami had its adhesive powder, other ships had electrified flooring, but the corridor surfaces of the Ng central command station possessed reverberating hummers.

The hummers sent activity data to a central computer that deployed scouts and police to investigate and eliminate possible threats to the station's safety. Thus, as Oteph stepped quietly down the hallway, flag in hand, he had no idea that his softly moving feet were being recorded far away in the command tower and that yet another patrol was headed their way. But he did not worry. Instead he stared blankly at his companions that sat shivering against the cold on a strange floor in a strange part of a planet they knew nothing about.

Oteph looked at them with a measure of pity. How interesting that such mighty creatures could be brought to nothing by the simple change in climate that the new surroundings afforded. Thaulab and Tovalu were the first to rise while Pierre and Bo'agg followed close behind. Security camera were present at nearly every corner of the complex. Oteph decided it was high time for him to use his new knowledge of computers to manipulate the cameras so that they showed images of their source rather than giving away his position.

The security command center was apparently located on level four, b-wing seventy-seven.

"Hey Val," he called, "take a look at this. Gobs and gobs."

"You're right, fat one, there's little time, we must get those guns."

Thaulab looked longingly at the scene on the monitor that showed a window that looked out on verdant pastures and a vast sea in the distance. "t each security station, the party looked upwards to monitor the presence of hostile guards and to find more information about the layout of the center. After hours of deliberated searching, the guard house was finally in view. Picking up weapons was easy, but fitting them to each differently shaped kweegon was difficult. Tovalu naturally request a large missile launcher, while Pierre and Bo'agg preferred simple laser pistols that they could hide in their breeches. "t long last, they were ready to move on . Oteph grabbed a portable scanner that would serve them as a navigational aid. The technology and science decks were located on floor three, but the main air-dock was located on nine deck, the tallest of the suspended surfaces.

Oteph seemed peaceful as he took up a position behind some rubbish. Fingering the tip of his whip, he sneered with what seemed to be pure greed at a fully loaded merchant ship that sat just on the opposite side of the deck being unloaded by a crew of dock workers. He glanced knowingly at the small band of Kweegons that he considered his friends. Thaulab bowed his head very slightly and placed his hand on the small laser pistol he had borrowed from the security locker.

Bo'agg and Pierre did the same while Tovalu took up a position that would allow a straight shot towards the service deck should the little pirates be seen. As fat and as clumsy as he was, Oteph could move silently as a feather when he needed to. On this occasion, he crept silently up the side of the launch pad. He drew within ten yards of the craft and then signaled for the rest of the party to follow.

The merchant ship was practically brand-new. It was of Andilaxian origin and, by its paint, belonged to the Inner Home system mercantile marine. A small ramp extended from the lower part of the storage bay to the floor where the workers were clearing cargo. It was not long before Oteph was noticed by security police that looked down upon the cargo shuttles and the men who worked there. Sirens flashed with purple and red lights while workers dropped their carts boxes and data tablets. Oteph rushed toward the ship waving to his companions to follow him. If he ever got the bird out of the dock he would be very happy. Unfortunately, he had no experience with the third-generation of Andilaxian ships.

The craftsmen of the Andilax system, had completed a set of controls that were uniquely suited for those of Igoilenat ancestry. But the Igoilenat were a hideous race with three-fingered paws, slobbery mouths and long, rat-like tails.

Oteph poured over the unfamiliar buttons of the main dashboard. So much had changed since the time of the Mon Ami and its primitive construction, that buttons had been redefined, scanner screens made into interactive holographic images. Luckily, it only took Thaulab and Tovalu the better part of thirty seconds to decipher the controls and set the ship on an escape route away from the docking station on Ng beta. The ploy worked in no small thanks to abilities of the Kweegons. Tovalu grasped the armrests of his command chair.

"I think we did it. Now to get past the guards." Tovalu frowned at he looked out at the ever-diminishing planet and then towards each horizon where there lay ten battle satellites ready to send them hurtling back to close orbital reach of the planet's air and defense force. Tovalu learned to use the guns of Andilaxian craft and these were no different. While he lay reflective chaff out of rear turrets, he trained the small merchant's missile turret toward one of the satellites. Within moments of impact, the small space weapon flashed momentarily and then was doused like candle pinched between two fingers. It was not long until Tovalu grew accustomed to the weapons console and, indeed, derived much pleasure in the pursuit.

Oteph sat dejectedly at the dashboard while he watched his fellows interact with the ship's computer creating a myriad of new defensive and offensive maneuvers every second that they were in view of a satellite. This was no Survey shuttle. This was a space craft. Oteph longed for the days when crashing down doors and slashing enemies in the face with his whip were the goal of the day. Oteph reason for being was now tied up in the future of these three little aliens. Every day he became less a Saurian and more a growing convert to the psychic determinism of the Kweegons. So they set out among the stars, not considering how far the tiny merchant would take them or if they had a chance of conquering the hated Igoilenat.

The Regiceld, for so it was called, was equipped with a slower than light propulsion unit that allowed the craft to travel up to half distances between a system's core or between a system and halfway to the next. Previous pilots of the ship had affectionately termed it the Halvsy, but their undying devotion to the Regiceld was solid. The Regiceld was heavily armored for its size, completely shielded against psychic attack and the use of astral projections. Its kweegon pilots, however meant to reprogram the shielding units to reflect amplified psychic force fields toward enemies and to cause catastrophic system failure in approaching hostile ships. The idea was ingenious and Pierre smiled for weeks after he had come up with the thought. It took weeks of hard , sweaty work until Oteph was able to rewire the ship's defensive shielding system. During this time, the ship lay vulnerable to even the smallest passing dust particle. Thus, Bo'agg and his elder brother Tovalu formed a canopy across all parts of the ships exposed hull. It wasn't much, but it protected the ship while repairs were being made. A stolen ship is no welcome guest at a star port.

Once the Regiceld was repaired, modified and otherwise improved, it was time to move into a regular schedule of upkeep and embarking on the journey to the Home planet of the Igoilenat. Comforted by the success of his repair job, Oteph began to eat more and gained weight. Unfortunately, the galley served a double role as a cargo hold and was, at the time, completely filled with boxes of metal ore. He observed how a pull-away section in the wall could be utilized as a ramp. He went away dejectedly and more hungry than ever.

Weeks passed as the merchant ship lumbered out of the Ng system and into deep space. Here in the world between the worlds, Oteph and his crew could see the wisdom of the universe. Four corners came together at this one juncture, the Igoilenat main system of Home. The Andilaxian, Saurian and Xerxian peoples all came to this place as common ground. It was a place of paradise for space pirates. Oteph smiled at the prospect of some thievery or at least some dancing about where money and life hangs in the balance.

"Can't we stay? We need better stuff than this," he said while waving a hand at the computerized weapons console.

"True. We do need that, but, most of all, we need you," Tovalu said in a deep growling voice, "We need you as our pilot."

Oteph understood what he meant, but stealing was his bag Direct confrontation with naval ships of one of the great civilizations of the realm didn't impress him.

"We're running low on fuel We need to stop," Oteph answered, "Once we drop this shipment, we can find another more important cargo." Oteph grinned through his yellow-stained teeth.

"Anyway, right here that's where we'll go, Org delta one. It's a moon. They have a port, women, booze and guns, the works." So the intrepid and unafraid crew directed themselves to the tiny star system that lay just out of Igoilenat space.

By this time, the Andilaxian ships were becoming more common just as the incidence of the Xerxian and Saurian ships started to dwindle. "t last, the Regiceld needed more fuel and got some on the asteroid, Mdukai. Oteph walked about the dusty ground and looked skyward to his home star , Pleay-beta three. He felt a wave of guilt rush over him. After the conquest of Home, the Kweegons intended to turn their eyes and tentacles toward Pleay and the Saurian civilization. First things first. Tovalu nervously guided his tentacles over the controls of the dashboard. The Regiceld had been hailed by an observer.

"Hail, Regula-Regiceld, state your numbers and your purpose." Tovalu remained silent at the console and broadcast over the communicator. "Regula Regiceld. Hey, answer guys! You've got no business here if you can't talk." Once again, Tovalu remained in deep contemplation and filled the line with perfect static. "Regula, you must respond or be attacked and forced to land." "t this point, Tovalu knew what he would do. He spun the ship around until its hard points were trained on the source of the security transmission. Oteph took the signal from Thaulab and rushed down the corridor to the docking bay. In moments, the ship's boat appeared from beneath the main hull and the heavily armored and armed ship started to pelt the security station with tight surgical blasts. With one final missile drop, the station was obliterated with only a billowing structural frame lefty behind.

"Get out of there!" Tovalu screamed at Oteph in the boat. Oteph had swung forward to see the damage in detail and to perhaps reconnoiter the possibilities of an impromptu base or redoubt. After all, fighting the Igoilenat is something that many had tried and failed at. Further, as the team aboard the Regiceld approached Home, they intercepted news and political broadcasts. Everywhere, nations panicked at the psychic forecast that predicted the coming of Visitors to Home. Children and adults fumbled with psi-shielding helmets, called brain boxes by the elite who did not think they needed them

The hysteria over Visitors did not limit itself to Home planet proper, but rumors and fear spread to the six moons and asteroid communities in the outlands. But hysteria also spread to the presidential council of military endeavors. New weapons were rolled out immediately. Since hi-tech weapons had proved useless against telepathic creatures in the past. Home gathered together the most ancient of its conventional warring squadron. thousands of bombers, localized nuclear bombs weather controlling devices all brought together the sum of Home's defenses. The sight of all the pitiable and ancient weapons caused the people to weep for their own despair and the death of their race.

Home was governed by two thousand local tyrants, three of which were absolute. In the time of the Visitor's attack, the tyrants glued themselves together to form armies that would save their common assets and insure a familiar future for all parties involved.

Oteph slopped himself across a cabin chair as he watched the scanners as they feeding data into the Radinon 3 about Home, its atmospheric content, its ability to sustain life for like and its habitability for oxygen breathing life.

1"Well," he said indicating the scanner, "Whatever's down there, we're sure gonna kill the Hell out of it."

"Study it," hummed Tovalu.

"OK, then we kill it"

"I don't know why we don't just go and tie you up again."

Oteph glanced at the screen and silently thought to himself. Tovalu who sat behind the navigation console made frequent use of the computer to adjust the ability of the ship to use psychic warfare. The Regiceld now had the capability of projecting small ships, scows and fighters in medium to long range distance from attacking ships. Just like Oteph was proud to have repaired the psi-shielding, Tovalu was proud of his equally important work on the computer. He felt every bit the genius that Patricia I must have been when she modified a mark 2 ship's computer into that which would equal the power of a mark 3. Tovalu, on the other hand, started with the Mark 3 computer but he was able to modify it to the standards of the common mark fives that were so common nowadays.

Home system was different from most systems of charted space. It was at the exact nexus of all five great races and it was also home to many of the most habitable planets in any one system in any region of space. Home was the living space of many different races from the rat like Igoilenat to the horse like-Jhounyms that lived on Home beta seven. Myriads of oceanic life teemed within the seas of Home and "dshastra. Frozen methane coated many lifeless asteroids, but the flying boulders were still home to some of the most valuable mineral veins in the galaxy. Interstellar trade was well developed within the realm of the Home system and it was easy to see why scientific studies of the Outland were so odd and interesting. In fact, it was the interstellar trader that created the stir in high society of Igoilenat culture. The approach of a merchant ship was always the source of much excitement and intrigue that citizens gazed heavenward whenever they had a chance to. However, the Regiceld was no welcome guest. As soon as the word came around that it was a visitor ship, Home's outer defenses were sealed and intercepting warships were dispatched. As with the Mon Ami, fully outfitted system ships were no match for the enhanced Regiceld that darted, dashed, listed and warped all the while picking apart the opposition with the clever piloting of Oteph, the sheer concentration of the lesser Kweegons and the mad navigational techniques of Tovalu. Within moment of the Igoilenat attack, the space lanes were quiet again, and the crew of the Regiceld looked toward Home, their destination in a week or more. It was at such times that Thaulab and the children would huddle closely in the bridge and communicate with Radinon, plotting a more perfect course.

With Home's defenses all but gone and planet wide hysteria already set well in, The crew of Regiceld, the Visitors, slowly approached the impending doom of yet another civilization. The constant hum of the thruster drive and the whirring of the oxygen freshers made for a certain amount of pre-invasion tension. Thaulab leaned back in his captain's chair and folded his hands together. Home was still months away , but it already appeared as a bright gem against the deep black of space.

Deep space allowed for certain absolutes and these were, the speed of the half-drive, the speed of light through the dark recesses of space and the certainty of habitable worlds. Home and Ng were companion stars. revolving around each other, planets of one system often dipped into the realm of the other. Ng bet seven often drifted toward Home whereas Home delta one was so small and so far from Home's core, that it actually became part of the Ng system on a regular basis.

The rotations of the two suns were a mystery to Oteph, but his crew mates took the discrepancies in stride It was there that the Regiceld found itself, lacking fuel, oxygen and food. And yet again, they had to leave empty with dirty duel in the tanks, decayed food in the galley and more than a little recycled water.

Once again, it was time to run. with only a half supply of refined fuel, they would have to go out of system to collect the things they needed. The plan was made to go into Xerxian space, a neighboring world on the edge of the kweegon realm. Oteph looked at the dash with wonder as he tried to decipher the movement of the planets. Looking at the universe from the smallest planet in the Ng/Home system was more difficult than it looked. Oteph had learned to manage the controls of the small freighter, but he was unsure of most of the powerful functions thereof. He came to trust in and befriend Tovalu. It wasn't easy for him to need a friend, because he lived so long as a hated parasitic creature since the time that he stole the Salvulent. As Oteph sat motionless at the dash, he secretly eyed Tovalu. He'd never had a friend, at least not long enough to express his own faithfulness.

Oteph viewed Thaulab, Pierre, Bo'agg and Tovalu as his friends. After years hating everybody, not knowing anybody and neither wanting to know. It was going to be hard, but Oteph knew he had found a place in life after all. Thaulab seemed to approve of his constant progress in the area of mind control and an ever deepening of his knowledge of the ship's systems. Soon, he was creating new algorithms for Radinon Four, plotting courses within and without Ng and was finally beginning to accurately track the Igoilenat trade routes and how they operated. However, attacking Home was no longer an option. Floating like a tiny cork on top of a basin of water, The Regiceld was not properly outfitted for corsair duties, but with Oteph the captain, the hijacking of trade returned to normal. Oteph us was happy, Thaulab was thoughtful and Tovalu and the rest were guardedly optimistic.

Within two months, The Visitors had captured three fighters, forty decatons of cargo and stymied the Ng navy as many times as they tried. If it was important for the Kweegons to capture and assemble an army of their own, it was equally imperative that trade be done with other pirate communities. The Regiceld, was, after all, a merchant and not a corsair as were some of the newly hijacked vessels. The Kweegons traveled in a rotating formation to prevent the possibility of attack by legitimate traders and warships.

In these days of closeness to Andilaxian space, Oteph left the console for meals and to relieve himself. The former, he managed to sneak on the bridge so he had something to munch on during the long hours of planning an entry into the Home system. They stayed in a holding pattern for months that seemed like years and eventually fell prey to people of their own ilk.

"bout six months from their internment at Ng, fleeing from system police, Oteph and the flotilla remained motionless in a turbulent crosswind of gravitational fields. They were powerless against the laws of space and nature and when he was about to give up, Oteph looked to Tovalu for some encouragement.

"Just keep it steady," he said, "I think I've got a fix."

This was good news, at least, because Oteph noticed the approach of five tiny specks on the down-looking dashboard. They had been found. Well, here we go again, he grunted. Placing the ship's systems on hold, he sprung from his seat and sped down the corridor to the communication shaft. Here, Tovalu, Bo'agg, Pierre and Thaulab stood waiting for him.

"Your word?"

"Battle stations," he said, barely looking up from the floor. Tovalu's lithe body shot through the hatch and was followed by the shorter Pierre and Bo'agg. Thaulab took his time entering the shaft. He seemed to be physically weak from some sort of malady. Whatever it was and whenever it happened, Oteph didn't care. Soon the flotilla of ships was activated and began to swarm around the approaching fighters.

When attacking hostiles, Oteph had learned the combat trade secrets of the Kweegons. Flying in a loose diamond configuration, the Kweegons were better able to project false images and intimidate the attackers into thinking they were attacking a massive navy when they were, in fact, fighting an old merchant ship, two fighters and a cargo scow. An astral projection of the barge transformed it into a corsair with heavy armament and ability to out maneuver any small attack ship in the galaxy. The truth was, however, that the scow had only one defensive sand caster and an even smaller laser cannon. It was well-suited to its purpose, but it was not suited for battle. Thaulab and his men remained in a secondary triangle behind Oteph and

Tovalu. It was there that they, the barge and the younger Kweegons set about to attack the computers of the oncoming ships. This was the most familiar type of warfare that Kweegons ever practiced. Once inside a computer, they could absorb all of the ship's data, navigational settings and targeting projections. Thus, it was a frolicsome pass time to watch the humanoid pilots try to shoot each other in the sky. The only problem was with the damaged equipment that had to be disposed of after the battle. Kweegons were smart, but they always left some kind of trail of wrecked ships, hollowed out space ports.

"t the end of the battle, the barge had taken the hardest hits of all leaving it listing precariously far from the Regiceld that had been ambling forward at a snail's pace while the battle raged.

"Where the hell were you guys?" Oteph yelled as he saw Pierre, Bo'agg and Tovalu entering the ship, "Can't I get any support? Just for once? Huh!" Oteph's face was red with anger.

"Your problem is...your anger O fat one," a relaxed Thaulab said. Pierre and Bo'agg stayed around long enough to blow their snouts at him and then departed to the galley where the rest of the "family" was dwelling in small but growing hives.

"We had to stay back. It's customary. It's how we work."

"Customary to leave me among those savages," Oteph snorted.

"Clearly you haven't learned," Thaulab said quietly and mournfully, "Perhaps we cannot teach you."

Thaulab' soft voice always burned Oteph. Generally always correct, he had said the truth this time. He must learn to control his anger, concentrate on the good of the Kweegons race and to let go of who he was as an individual, obstreperous, self-involved pirate. To him, the thought of it was crushing and to perform that which was needed was even more foreign to him. Oteph looked at his boots and shuffled down to the galley where he met the youngest of the Kweegons. They were easier to be around. They didn't judge, they didn't correct and they certainly couldn't discern him from any other person aboard. Oteph was only at home in a cloud of lies and with the younger ones, he could be whoever he wanted to be.

Reaching an escape vector into the Home system took quite some time, but eventually the flotilla managed to safely drift into the neighboring system without fear of being drawn back to Ng.

Home system differed much from Ng in that three of its planets were more or less habitable. Of those, two, Gocuda and Heewheg were water world, the former an ice capped barren globe while Heewheg was a balmy, highly humid ocean world. The largest and most advanced of Home's planets was Gyukk, a planet with habitable regions, agricultural commodities, mineral deposits, food and even refined fuel. Luckily Gyukk was their next stop before heading on towards the waterworlds and the asteroid belt that ringed Home like a wide leather girdle.

"Is it time?" Oteph said as he looked at Thaulab. Getting an affirmative nod, he signaled to Tovalu that the landing process was to begin. The merchant ship had a small planetary boat, but Oteph and the crew expected trouble. Thus, the barge and two fighters were sent to the planet's surface to retrieve food and fuel and hopefully to offload some cargo from the vast holds of the Regiceld.

"Gyuuk was home to some of the finest amenities known to local and deep space, thus the importance of her capture. The barge and the two fighters set down easily on a port that looked over vast roiling sea. The landing pad stood far above the surface of the planet, but supplies and trade were able to be transferred without undue interaction with the planet's normal state of affairs. It was a cargo factory. Large load-bearing robots relieved the barge of its contents while individual cart-masters inspected the fuel holds of the two fighters. Pierre and Bo'agg, two young pilots looked on

as their ships were being examined, poked
and prodded. As for the barge, it was quickly
loaded with fuel and ready to return to low
orbit about the planet. Pierre and Bo'agg
could not believe that the task could have
been so simple, and yet it wasn't. As soon as
the barge left the pad, dock workers turned
to look at them. Pierre and Bo'agg had used
a false projection of themselves to hide their
identities and thus they looked like ordinary,
shorter-than-usual, swarthy Andilaxian
Igoilenat.

"Hey. Who are you guys?" One of the men
asked. Bo'agg began to shake uncontrollably.
He had never been this close to a humanoid.
Oteph was the only non-kweegon life form
he'd ever seen and even he, the slobbering lazy
lump, was not a very good representation.

"We're here to barter for supplies and fuel,"
Bo'agg could feel his skin growing warmer by
the minute. Beads of sweat began to gather
on his soft hide and as his fear grew, his
camouflage began to flicker and he started
to appear as an alien to those on the deck.

"Wait!" he yelled, "You're a visitor come to
bleed us dry. The dock master was a short,
sweaty young man who carried a pipe in his
hand and a large metal beam in the other.
His eyes blazed with anger, "You killed my
father."

Bo'agg began to panic all over again. Who
was his father and why should I care, he

thought. Pierre stood boldly by the side of his friend.

"We don't know your foolish talk, savage. We come in peace, but could depart in war." Pierre seemed to derive pleasure at making the dock masters angry. He smiled to himself.

"Bloody visitors. Just come to destroy me."

"Kweegons, actually," he said, "We just want what's ours and we'll leave you in peace, maybe."

Thirteen

Since the dock masters stood resolute in their defense against those whom they called visitors the two glanced hopefully toward the fighters. Bo'agg and Pierre exchanged troubled glances.

I'm afraid they suspect. Got to get back somehow. Must tell master Tovalu.

"As they silently communicated, Pierre used his affectation to train one of the ship's lasers at the deck. As soon as the ship started firing, Bo'agg and Pierre ran for cover and heaved themselves up the side of the star fighters. Within minutes, both crafts were airborne and systematically destroying the port one section at a time. When the port was no more than a burning shard of metal and composite, system defense boats seemed to appear from nowhere. From low tech fighter jets to fusion caterpillar-driven sky trucks, they all converged on Pierre and Bo'agg as they were destroying the last of the sky port.

Luckily, the Ng craft was more nimble and light than were the system defense forces and a relatively easy escape was possible with only a small bit of concentration.

But Bo'agg wasn't the experienced pilot that Pierre was. Too many hours in recreation and the galley had left his mind soft and his belly continually larger and more needy. It was not long before the Gyuuk navy caught him in a tailwind and sent him hurtling through the atmosphere to the ocean below. It was humiliating but since he was slack in his studies as a pilot he deserved such a fate. He managed to ditch his craft before it slammed into the waves. In due time, he found himself in the water. "t one with the water Kweegons were creatures of humidity and not so much of swimming or water activities. In much the same way that his fellows had summoned and commandeered merchants, science boats and warships, he conjured for himself a picture of the ocean: that which was below, all around him and what size.

Gyuuk appeared to be home to an almost infinite array of sea life. From tiny plankton to giant large-mouthed univors. Spread eagled on the top of the waves, remained still until someone would happen by. He had to make it to a port or he would die on this hostile savage planet.

Kweegons like Bo'agg were creatures of humidity and not so much of swimming or water activities. In much the same way that his fellows had summoned and commandeered merchants, science boats and warships, he conjured for himself a picture of the ocean: that which was below, all around him and what size.

Gyuuk appeared to be home to an almost infinite array of sea life. From tiny plankton to giant large-mouthed unvors. Spread eagled on the top of the waves, remained still until someone would happen by. He had to make it to a port or he would die on this hostile savage planet. Bo'agg sank out of consciousness and the sea that then was swallowed him like a dead fish.

Bo'agg awoke in a new world, one in which he was once a native. Swimming idly with the currents, he communicated with the plants, algae and kelp. It was like home to a Kweegon, but having never seen or experienced the Hive, every new thing was like an epiphany, each day like an age of the universe. Bo'agg forgot his masters. The memories Thaulab, Pierre and the pirate slipped from his memory. And he began to reproduce. First, in small fits in which his body trembled cramped and then relaxed. His life swayed with the tide as he settled to the floor of the ocean becoming one with the rocky crags and shifting sands of time. It was here that his hands and feet felt at home in a state of weightlessness.

"As time passed, Bo'agg grew and his substance became a rocky crag that spread quickly along the sea's bottom. Small fish and plankton sought refuge in his wispy leaves as they were hunted by larger prey. Bo'agg changed the fish. They grew. Bo'agg's fish became large as unvors and as peaceful as evobeetles that skittered along the ocean's floor. Bo'agg's fish became large and his spirit inhabited them. His first contact with the Igoilenat occurred as his creatures began to walk on land. Bewildered as ever, the new Kweegons--visitors encountered the Igoilenat quite by accidents. Dangling damp feet in a warm pool of salty water, two of the young were drinking up the beauty of a new civilization on the barren , lifeless planet.

"Who are you?" a voice behind them demanded. The creatures that were Bo'agg's young slowly changed their countenances to that of the humanoid savages. "n attractive man and a woman both about thirty-ish and dressed in leisure costumes gingerly turned toward the Igoilenat who stood astounded by the shift of appearance. "What seems to be the trouble," asked the female in light, almost musical tones.

"I...uh..I'd rather you not be here," the astonished Igoilenat answered.

"Why?" asked the man in feminine sounding tones, "Whatever could be wrong?"

"Well, I suppose we must move along," the female said as she sprung upon the male Igoilenat. In a flash, the "female" Kweegon had jumped on the man holding his head firmly upon her tentacled hands. It was not long before the man's body slumped to the ground lifeless and as white as the sky. The male and female of Bo'agg's shifted into an eerily green wisp and the two coalesced into one solid green form that came further ashore shifting like candle shadows from tree to tree in the forest and from scrub to grass in the clearings. Meanwhile, Pile's spirit grew enveloping the world of the undersea.

With each new triumph of kweegon over the natives, Bo'agg continued to grow along the surface of the deep. His body became wispy and soft and where his loins used to be there grew a small hive where new children were created every moment that his emissaries were on land and in the midst of Igoilenat culture.

The triumph over the Igoilenat of Gyuuk had its setbacks. The Igoilenat were individual thinkers and soon went into hiding against the visitors. Families of the Igoilenat clung together in hopes that the Kweegon threat would go away while scientists and librarians searched for ways of dealing with the outlanders. For years, survey crews and warships had encountered and dealt with the creatures and their hive mentality by using fragmentation weapons. "lone they were just weak pieces of a very large puzzle. It was only the chaotic nature of a subject race that could conquer such peoples. The question remained

Winston Sharp clenched his fists as he looked through the archive scanner. It was an occupation that normally filled the most pleasurable hours of his day. He loved the quietness of the archives. And the shielding they afforded him from the rest of the world. They were his escape. In a time when his peers had found families and children, he had sought and found some corners of the galaxy. After the alert and general panic at the landing of the visitors, Winston was the most sharp and quick with finding information on the creatures.

"What've you got for me Doctor," a tense voice asked over the sagging shoulder of the elderly teacher.

"Best that I can see is that they're the same bunch that destroyed the Spiral Serpent and the Mon Ami so many years ago. we've got our hands full here."

"Is there not anything we can do," the man said.

"No, Mark, judging by the time and how many are actually reproducing on land, the oceans must be literally teeming with the creature, if there is only one. I must study some recent data together information about their current tactics, they're very smart, you know."

"I know," Mark said resignedly, "You can get more information about that from satellite seven if you want. "Normally, this would be fun, but we're past that now. We must change or die."

Fourteen

Winston nodded his head slowly and turned again to the archival scanner. Placing knowledge and facts together, he hoped to find the secret behind the Spiral Seven and the wreck of the Mon Ami. The history of the latter was most interesting because it involved a team of scientists that Winston had known at Gymnasium. Patricia I Buonaparte was the head of her class. Genius material. Even Winston with his reclusive style and vast encyclopedic knowledge could not process and solve problems as fast as she. Patricia I had met these visitors and died in the process. Her legacy was the Radinon Three. Made from the shambles of an ordinary ship's computer, her creation was the first major small-scale defense against these psychic creatures that fed on knowledge and on the souls of sentient creatures.

Winston thumbed his nose as he looked at the screen. How could we succeed where this genius failed, he asked himself. Winston remembered that he was needed on an appointment. "n appointment of the heart with a woman that was not needed or attractive by his own taste. He would rather stay in his lair, especially at this dire hour. With Bo'agg growing stronger and more numerous with each passing moment, The Igoilenat of this outpost needed a scientist and not a lover of women. He worked feverishly over the keyboard of the scanner hoping to find some, if any, evidence of a weakness in these creatures. "t any rate, Home must be warned.

Not three months into their long journey to Home, the crew of the Regiceld had settled into a slow and steady pace that seemed like a virtual ramble among the planes of a vast system.

"The ones they call Igoilenat are more blessed than they think," Oteph murmured, " even among what they call 'barren' there is more life than in the sum of Xerxians."

"Yes. Perhaps they don't deserve their good fortune," Tuvalu spoke as though he were caught in a trance. The Regiceld had many things of benefit not the least of which was a hanging navigational bar.

Now that the flotilla was closing quickly upon the planet Home, an almost perfect arc could be seen between the prison planet Our and the new destination, Home the plane of the Igoilenat.

"Don't you ever think about Bo'agg?" Oteph suddenly said as he spun his chair lazily about.

"No." "answered Thaulab curtly, " No. I do not and neither should he. You and I agreed upon this once. Had you forgotten?"

"Didn't forget. just missing a friend."

"Our friend, Bo'agg has his job to do and ours. Soon we'll be at Igoilenat and, if they are as ready for us as the Xerxians were at Shaking, we'll be in trouble. We need more ships, more firepower."

"Yeah, but you can use your minds, right? Just light up the place with fairies?"

Not always. We couldn't do that with you. You are Saurian and have innate defenses that none of the others have. You are the elite among the physical warriors. Yes, indeed. We'll have need of you

Thaulab massaged his chin and snout while he turned again to the console where Tovalu was glowering over the active navigation computer. Feeling more than a little rebuked, Oteph turned back to his duties as well. Oteph looked at the dash where he sat and suddenly began to cry. He knew where Bo'agg had gone to. He knew what he did and he knew he was unnecessary to the mission with his Saurian . Bo'agg cursed himself and then as if by magic, her heard the deep sonorous voice of Thaulab.

Do not sigh or cry, fat one, you must guide us to the places of governance of the Igoilenat. None of the hive can stay stable that long. Well, true. You are fat and greasy, your movements slow and deliberate, but you are our hope.

Oteph felt his heart sink within him. " humanoid assisting others to kill his own kind? He had not felt so wretched since the time he crashed in on a mother and her sleeping babe and chopped them to pieces with his small strength blade. Thaulab seemed to understand the trouble that Oteph felt and tried to help.

"The Igoilenat hate you, Oteph. They've hated you longer than they knew you existed," he said, "They will kill you if they can. Your only hope is with us. We must destroy them."

Oteph felt a warm sense of affirmation when Thaulab talked. It was a warm sort of feeling that assured him that all was going to be well. The last months aboard the Regiceld had been crucial for him. He had learned to trust his friends and the Hive that now grew unchecked in the rear of the craft. In fact, the Hive was the Regiceld because the small collection of young that Thaulab had deposited there nearly a year ago had grown into a living presence that only the central Radinon had power over. The Hive now determined the fate of the Igoilenat and Home. They were weeks away from planet fall.

The weeks fell away like the dried leaves on the shrubs of Saurus. Oteph was often caught in a reverie about his days in his home, the departure from Saurus and the years of whore mongering and banditry that followed. The Wreck of the Salvulent symbolized for him the closure of a chapter in his life where life was free and so were the women, money and lechery of all sorts. Oteph learned that the easy way out of trouble dwelt in his now-empty hip-pocket.

President Winston Sharp took another slurp of coffee before he peered over the archive monitors at a small, but impressive city officer. Hugo Brinx was a planetary guardian of sorts.

"What is it," Winston asked with a slight bit of irritation.

"Sir," he quavered, "The astronomy reports. Mac from Gyuuk reports presence and infestation of visitors. The oceans are nearly covered and the things keep getting bigger. Now, the entire oceanic floor is nearly covered by the greenish pollution. There are rumors of a second wave of visitors."

"And somehow I must stop them."

"If you put it that way, yes. They must be stopped." Winston frowned, slurped hungrily at his coffee and then turned to face the window that looked out upon the city, such as it was. Hugo could be the most irritating wretch he knew, but this time he was right. Lord Racine remained as the sole hope of his people. The times called for the soft-spoken tyrant and the people knew it. Soon, Racine's face was found everywhere. Large placards and monuments declared "Unite as One!" "others said, "The Time is Now." It was all a part of quenching the paranoia of a rightfully scared public. Racine's weekly program became a daily broadcast propaganda and angst. Meanwhile, political underling scrambled to arrange for the orderly evacuation of an entire planet.

"Bury them in the earth," Winston mumbled to himself as he read the latest bulletin from the Protector's office. Home consisted of a vast desert belt and two polar temperate regions that accommodated minor seas , water ways and extensive system of underwater caverns

"The shielding is much better there," Hugo murmured softly.

"We couldn't live twelve months in there." Winston continued to look out the window as if the answers to Igoilenat survival depended on the gentle swaying of pine trees or the way a young man and his girl sat and kissed in the park. It made no sense.

"Already we have lost Gyuuk to these, these animals. What did you call them?"

"Visitors, sir. Just Visitors."

"Call Racine. Tell him that we will make for the underground caverns. It's our only chance." Hugo bowed and backed out of the room as he grabbed his phone from a leather pocket at his waist.

In the month before the landings, government leaders worked speedily to assign numbers and classification for every essential person in the world. The poor and lame were left above for lack of space and to save resources for those who would carry the species onward. For the outsiders, the Visitors' approach seemed both scary and mildly hopeful. They were a people abandoned by their own race. Who was to say that Visitors could be less barbaric.

Tomaaz' legs weren't old, but they were twisted and splayed outward in such a way that he needed to drag himself through life in a wooden cart with small metal wheels. Boiled, noxious liniment that was his daily treatment, had run out weeks ago since the last of the higher classes sought refuge in the caves. The empty cities had no medical supplies and certainly no doctors. So here he was writhing in constant agony, his spine and hips burning with fiery pain. That is when the sands came. Their heat b brought comfort to his bones and he often immersed himself in the soft, warm substance that increasingly blew in from the borderlands. Tomaaz was not the only one to survive the early selections. The poor had gathered themselves into groups. By the time the visitors came, they had become one.

Tomaaz sat by the door of his house, a small wooden box, rubbing the pain out of his ankles in preparation for another day of traveling through deserted streets searching for others. Like any other day, however, he would find Home northern quadrant 456 empty of anything except gamblers, rogues and various space trash that had come to stake a claim in the abandoned lands where he and his people lived. There were settlers from as far away as Ng system who must have headed for Home at the first news of the capture of the scout ship, Mon Ami. After a while, it was not hard to see why he had been left topside. The refugees of Home wandered from deserted hamlet to deserted town, country and region and everywhere there showed the emptiness of a land soon to be raped by outlanders, corsairs and pirates of the galaxy. Tomaaz thought of himself of something of a junk crab, scuttling from one home to another always leaving small wheel traces and waste in his trail. "t times the depression was too much. He would fling himself forward from his cart and with sand in his mouth and the upturned cart laying beside him, he would kicked it away in rage. The thickening layer of sands in the streets had nearly made it impossible to travel. Now was the time to hide.

Tomaaz' small drama was similar to that of most of the rejected few. Here and there a family that struggled under the tyranny of Lord Racine searched frantically for shelter and safe housing were cast out of places that they once thought were secure. The world was changing and they could not predict it and paid the consequences. By the thousands they were swept up and taken away as prisoners in their own homes.

The scientific community, ever at odds with the political community, had experienced crisis's like this before. Each new survey shuttle to make its long journey home was bound to discover and, in many cases, bring home alien life from other worlds, planets or other locales in space. The spider horse was one such oddity. Brought Home by a surveyor of the Andilax system, the spider horses were oxygen breathing arachnids. Because of their high trainability, they were soon adapted to agricultural and transport uses in low-tech ends of the system. Spider horses could carry immense amounts of cargo, goods and even passengers across deserted or even ice capped regions of desolate planets. The already tired Winston looked at the small man in front of him and frowned, "Now what does that have to do with me?'

"I thought you'd ask that. The Over Lord has answered the problem." Hugo jammed a crumpled piece of paper at Winston's face, "Here Read."

"What is it? " recipe? Sorry don't cook." Winston waved the tips of his fingers at Hugo and sniffed. "Hasn't it been years since we sent out a probe to Altair beta-one? What of those documents? We don't just throw those things up there for nothing." Winston felt his face flush as he thought of things brought on by an overactive political system. Hugo was simply a Paige, but he represented the only challenge that the Igoilenat had of reaching space under the care of basic science.

"The thing that lives on Gyuuk is benign. If anything, it was good for the population to increase its amount of greenery."

"Greenery!" Hugo shouted, equally upset, "The oceans are barren. The people are starved and those lucky enough to be left behind by the polluted land are contorted corpses. There's benign for you. Just listen what the man has to say." Hugo deftly tried to slip the paper under Winston's nose.

"Well, I suppose so, but there's nothing to be done."

"Alert the psi-shielders. Surely we must be able to block some of the invasion."

"psychic shielding only works in localized settings. We can't guard a whole planet."

"Then who do we leave behind? Who is useless and probably half-dead already?"

Hugo scratched his chin and started to speak and then stopped in mid-sentence, "Perhaps...the outlanders. But they have no laws."

"No." Winston said authoritatively. "Even those rebels have some code of order. Over Lord wants us to divide good from bad here. It's going to be impossible."

"and we have only a month..."

Home and her defenses were slow to assemble and, by the time that visitor flotilla had reached the asteroid belt that separated Home from all of the other habitable planets. Every day, the visitors inched closer and closer to the home of the Igoilenat. Hugo Brinx set to work notifying heads of state and allowing for the construction of shielded bunkers to be used in the event of an attack. Every civilized race had them. Primitive "Asunur who roamed the wastelands riding on spider horses had no provision whatsoever against the coming attacks. The "Asunur were a tribal people bound to each other by hatred of outsiders and the common feelings of homeliness provided by the vast stretches of nothing but harsh, barely livable landscape.

The Asunur were a tribe of many separate nations that survived off of the basic elements of life that could be found growing near water holes, small salty lakes and springs.

The nomadic tribes fed a constant hatred amongst themselves toward the Igoilenat. Tribal Lords not only competed with one another, but they also ransacked, raped and otherwise burgled outlying settlements of the poorest of the Igoilenat. For this, they earned a place of hatred among the governmental authorities. Hugo Brinx simply sniffed when Winston suggested they needed protection too.

"Let 'em rot. Useless bunch of spider herds." Winston winced when he heard the all-too-familiar sentiments coming from Hugo. After all, Hugo was a cog and a mouthpiece in the wheel of Igoilenat culture. He would soon lead the government into an era of self-protection the likes of which Home had never needed or seen

"but what about them? Their culture. Don't you see they're in danger, too?"

"Good. Then let's have done with them."

"Good."

Within a month, all heads of state were secluded in bunkers made from high density shielding materials. "complex communication system allowed political affairs to be conducted underground. Meanwhile, the "Asunur roamed emptied cities and deserted buildings. For ,any of them, the temperate zones were like an alternate reality. leaves grew on trees, tiny rivulets of water trickled softly and silently down public gutters. Each town and village was centered about a central monument, whether it be a plaza with stones, a cultic temple or colonnade. The "Asunur took up residence in empty houses, learned to wear cold-weather clothes and shoes. The spiders simply roamed the streets as their owners became more interested in the new land.

Fifteen

Not all Igoilenat were deemed qualified to be included in a shelter. Poor and sick lined many streets and alleys shivering and afraid of the encroaching Asunur. The Asunur were not a bad people. They traveled in pairs down the wide streets walking and sometimes riding. Years in the desert had made their eyes as sharp as those of the aero-revenants, the vermin of the sky. The Asunur were gaunt self-effacing creatures who peered down long streets and scientifically examined waste bins, cul-de-sacs and barrows. They readied themselves with the arms of the desert, small black pebbles and leather thongs. Highly pitched ocarinas and the occasional pointed reed. Always unshod, they moved quickly and silently. By the time the visitors came, The Asunur owned not only the desert, but the towns as well. It was with much curiosity that Chief Agwentuli, leader of the tribe looked upon the grizzled features of Oteph as he stepped off of Regiceld's landing boat.

The pair just watched each other apprehensively while prowling about the edges of the small plaza . Oteph felt beads of sweat gathering on his face merely due to the change in atmosphere of Home and that of the boat. Agwentuli, for his own part, looked disgustedly upon Oteph sloppy overweight features and the odor that surrounded him. Agwentuli reached for his reed and stood perfectly straight as though the reed caused his very persona to align itself with the dried wood.

"Tell your leader we have no need of him" Agwentuli spoke in a language that was slightly foreign to Oteph, but his psychic powers allowed him to hear them internally.

"This is our world, Igoilenat. Find your own or run from the daylight in the living tombs of stupid fear."

Oteph hoped the creature could hear his primitive Saurian as he said, "Their fears are not stupid, straw man, and I am no Igoilenat. I am from the ship Regiceld of the hive of Thaulab. I am Oteph, just a foolish bandit hard on his luck. We have come to take this planet and make of it our home. Your capitol will be a hive and your oceans the web."

The code of Asunur joined the ranks of those listening to the newly introduced kweegons. Silently they stood in columns behind Agwentuli as he continued to make his plea to Thaulab and Oteph. Thaulab seemed less interested in the words of Agwentuli as he was in the scenes about the city and he wondered at the faithfulness of this tribe to its leader. There was much to gain here and Thaulab wanted it to happen soon. Using his inherent communications, he learned the true meaning of the display

Sixteen

Oteph well knew the language of space travelers and was not surprised to see a primitive example of one here. That language was merely a mixture of the minority languages of the several systems along a trade route.

Ineic was one such language. Oteph did not speak Ineic but could reply in the primitive tongue of the Saurians which he had spoken since his youth. The language of space was the language of the pirates. Old Saurian existed for his purposes of plying the outer realms in search of repairable ships and money. Money mostly, and then the occasional woman friend. He turned to the Zepab and spoke in their language,

"Come with me to find the hated ones." As he spoke, he waved his hands upward at the top of the building encircled by glass windows but crumbling with age. The tribesman looked in wonder at the fat man standing before them helping them to find what they needed. Normally, the Igoilenat were terrified, here stood Oteph in his grandeur telling secrets that once been entrusted to him. Tovalu rose once and then lay down as the Zepab rushed by him with slings and pebble pouches swinging and rustling up the long staircase. He turned to look at Oteph who just shrugged his shoulders.

"You," he said as he fell back to the ground. Oteph immediately set to work on repairing the shuttle craft. The Zepab were far too interested in capturing yet another group of Igoilenat that they failed to see the danger of leaving Oteph behind.

Within an hour, Oteph had used the best of his strength to drag Tovalu back into the shuttle and lay him out in the double stateroom. From the long range laser communicator, Oteph contacted the Regiceld and was soon connected to the wizened face of master Thaulab.

Connected to local life forms. Igoilenat are poor pathetic creatures. Asunur roam the streets freely, don't respond well to reading. Tovalu injured...could be dying. I captured Igoilenat, killed them and rescued the boat. The spider walkers escaped.

Thaulab felt visibly angry and Oteph could feel the pulsating rage in his mind and body. Oteph, you must go. Take Tovalu. Return.

It was no small feat to get the boat operational again and by that time, the Zepab had returned with more improvised weapons found in the building. Bits of mortar and iron pelted the craft as it bravely lifted from the dust on which it lay and sped toward the sky. The Zepab scattered at the sound of the noise and the extreme heat of the exhaust thrusters.

On board the Regiceld, Thaulab came to greet the two scouts in the entryway to the airlocks. Oteph proudly strolled through the walkway while an injured Tovalu stumbled along bracing his huge body along the walls of the chamber. Thaulab looked at his navigator with pity and sent him directly to the galley where the hive had remained still since the landing of the ship's boat on Home.

"You did what?" one of the family asked, "And to who? Don't you know that Bo'agg only survived by allowing some to live. You've made enemies of both the tribes and the Igoilenat. In a short time, you have shown yourself worthless and pathetic." Oteph looked down at his browned, dirty boots.

"So...I suppose it's over."

"That right. Even if Tovalu recovers, we're stuck here in high orbit until food and oxygen run out."

Oteph looked at Thaulab for some encouragement, but all he got was a look of shame and disappointment

"I'll just...I'll just...go."

The hive worked day and night to revive the ailing body of Tovalu, but in the mean time, young Rubamen Copad and Jafo Ebutub assumed the positions as commander and navigator. Managing a flotilla of out-dated space barges and merchants through deep space was a daunting task in itself, but for two young fliers the challenge of maintaining the same group in far orbit around a planet was nearly impossible and for this, they were given the watchful eye of Thaulab until the time arrived to once more attempt a landing

With Oteph sequestered in the brig, It was a time of panic aboard the Regiceld. As Thaulab watched intently the data recordings that came from the planet, he directed his young pupils in the art of surveillance. The Igoilenat were of course invisible to the computers, but Thaulab could feel them moving in each nerve of his body. His tentacles twitched as panicked cries went out from shelter to shelter about the terrible Asunur and the aliens who helped them destroy an entire community of citizens. Oteph's presence on the mission had created unforeseen problems and now it was a battle against time.

The Igoilenat had legions of fighting men and machines that had never been tested against the spider riding nomads and despite their undying hatred and apprehension of the wilderness tribes, organized efforts against them had never been made. For the most part, Igoilenat concentrated its energies on the advancements of science, politics and religion. Their missions to the stars were conducted yearly and the failure of some teams to return caused fear and yet the tribes of the wilderness never changed and neither did their skirmish-based society.

Deep in the midst of Home's remaining organized government secret plans were made to reemerge from hiding and expel the hated Asunur and perform an organized attack upon the Kweegons should they return.

Seventeen

Months after the first incursion of the visitors to the border of the civilized regions of Home, the underground political machine took basic steps to return to the surface and ward off any lingering phobias that the populace had over the psychic race.

Overlord Stavro Racine introduced a new program of sorting the planet into habitable portions versus the overrun quarters where fellow unprotected citizens were hunted and killed by the Zepab and various other tribes. Lord Racine in the general moot called for the resurrection of the Army and flying forces to battle the imminent threat of invasion. Since the war machines were largely robotic and mechanized, the populace was comforted to know that their welfare lay in the artificial hands of disposable robot mechanisms. Army "foot soldiers" were in reality small boxes on wheels that sported a daisy-wheel type of weapons platform. Mostly the soldiers shot at rustling leaves or rolling bushes. That was how they were programmed and could do no more. Racine ordered the dispatch of some eighty million combat robots to roam the streets of border settlements and kill every Asunur that they encountered. After a month of robotic war, the Igoilenat returned. Lords and their ladies resumed their duties in the manner that they once knew. The Asunur, driven away by constant slaughter retreated to the far reaches of the deserted land taking spider horses, modern guns and food with them. It was time to rebuild for the wanderers and they knew it.

Lord Racine was first to suggest that the robot purges were a great success and recommended further mechanization of all life processes and needs. The military robots figured heavily into the new society while all other robotic forms like the agricultural and psychotherapeutic operated in close proximity to the actual citizenry. What Lord Racine called the "resurrection" began among the wealthiest of the citizenry and led to the eventual resettlement of civilized regions of the globe. Everywhere, images of Hugo Brinx could be seen on television or on news transmissions.

As Jafo and Rubamen continued to monitor the actions on Home's surface, they observed the growing reliance on the electronic rather than the psychic. "new sortie was ripe. "t the time of the resurrection, the Hive quivered with a new and perhaps indulgent joy that could only be appreciated by the young ones and possibly Oteph who still lay restrained in a locked cell next to the galley. Some fine mess this is, He thought, a civilization brought to its knees by an unknown threat. Him. Oteph was sure it was him. He struggled night and day against the straps that kept him safely from interrupting or communicating with the hive or the ship's Radinon which it now controlled. Thus, it was a great surprise when the door of his sell slid haltingly open and a tired, gray-headed Thaulab peeked his head through the door.

"Oteph, I've seen you walking these corridors at night. We might be able to use you again. Don't hurt my people. We could make peace with these...Igoilenat."

"Make peace," he said hoarsely but angrily, "Is that what you did for the Mon Ami: Rafael, Patsy. You can no more make peace than destroy an entire world by sitting on it."

"Not what I meant. My troops, if can call them that, have never used primitive weapons. All we want is a place to ourselves and Home is perfect. Then we need not keep searching for a place. At this time, Bo'agg still battles for his own existence on a planet thought uninhabitable by the Igoilenat and yet they dare keep their wastelands as well as their civilized regions away from us. We deserve it. It's ours and we'll keep it

Oteph noticed that Thaulab's countenance changed as he talked of the imminent takeover of Home. From the pleasant old wise man he turned into what seemed like a grasping greedy wretch. His skin blanched as he talked of the next mission and he clenched his fists and jaw as he mentioned the Asunur and how they would be removed. He was not a kweegon at all. He was a conqueror here to get what he thought he deserved. This being so, he rejoined the crew, a new boat was prepared. and he and a few of Vneezl the young ones made the long slow drop into Home. Closing in on the borderlands, the commander set the boat down in between two massive, sandblasted buildings. It seemed that where the Asunur didn't conquer, the desert itself did.

Oteph stepped off the platform with his shoulders held high. His arms felt strong and he walked with the swagger of someone who owned the world. After all, he did. No one could challenge him in dealing with the Asunur. The team had touched down in the middle of a small sandstorm and Oteph was the only one sufficiently protected to walk out onto the planet's surface. Urban sandstorms were more common now that the Asunur had discovered the comforts of the city. Tree, shrubs and grass grew into debris and blew away into the desert and after several months, the tree-lined streets became sand-laden dunes. By virtue of his great strength, Oteph pulled the boat in between two buildings and there he rested until the rest of the team was equipped. Vneezl stood on the precipice of the exit plank wearing a black and yellow heavy armor suit. Oteph laughed at the site of it because nowhere were the Kweegons known to wear armor of any kind. They didn't need it with their psychic abilities. Vneezl, barely fifty years old looked foolish in the suit. His eyes barely reached the base of the helmet and his tiny fingers were too small to manipulate the gauntlets on each arm, but he more than made up for the deficiency in the possession of an anhydral impact hammer that he had strapped to his back. Obviously the spoils of some venture into Xerxian space, the great hammer glowed dimly in the weak light of Ng and its neighbor-star Home. The double shadow produced by the two suns made him feel proud and larger than he actually was. He fingered the hammer gingerly and then skipped down the plank to join Oteph who was also looking warily about him. Thaulab and the recently recovered Tovalu were the next group to descend to the surface of the sandy street. Tovalu was also clothed in heavy armor with a much smaller hammer and Thaulab wore only a lab tunic preferring to deal; with the Igoilenat with bare-hands, as it were. The team took temporary refuge in a building close to where they had landed and waited for the approach of the slow moving arachnids or the occasional passage of Igoilenat security bots.

According to Vneezl's monitoring of the sector, they had landed in the most populated area in the anterior pole of the land mass called the great Virdimm. t was a place not unlike any other great depression of a land continent. All civilized and habitable areas were at or below the altitude of the sea. Thus, water spouts and natural springs provided occasional water to the desert and maritime climes as well. The Virdimm had been intensely studied ever since the Regiceld had been two months away from Home orbit and now it had been six additional months until Tovalu and Thaulab were prepared to embark on the second sortie into the realm of the Asunur and Igoilenat. The burden of knowledge had been placed squarely on the weak shoulders of the young Vneezl who barely stood several inches higher that Oteph himself. The long adventure of preparation was over. He could feel his skin drying within his suit and he felt all the weaker for it. Sensing the trouble, Tovalu grabbed Vneezl by the back of his armored thorax and said,

"You'll have to adjust the oxygen, stupid." As Vneezl watched carefully, Tovalu adjusted some of the diodes on the chest plate of the suit. Almost instantly, the world seemed cooler, moister and clearer. Vneezl felt free to look about the area, to smell the dusty, abandoned atmosphere and to touch through his gauntlet sensors the sandblasted edges of the buildings.

Eighteen

The group was assembled for a small foray into the dried and deadened atmosphere. With Oteph and his electro-flag leading the way, Vneezl, Tovalu and Thaulab led the way through the deserted streets and yellow buildings. The city was a ruins, but place names were still available to those who sought after them. It was not long before the team entered a dusty field with a destroyed gazebo at its center, concrete benches lined the four corners of the field and once excellent marble had disintegrated into crushed gravel.

"'" town center," Oteph mumbled softly.

"The answer is here. The Town Hall," Vneezl said.

As the team of visitors searched the field for more clues, they discovered that the place had also been used recently as a nest for the Zepab. Spider feces was spread incongruously throughout the field, but was most concentrated near the gazebo. This must have been their Hive," Thaulab murmured. Vneezl, Tovalu and Oteph ascended the stairs that led to the center stage . From there they could clearly see the streets that extended in concentric circles from the center. The city had apparently been built around a specific point in the park.

"But where do we start," a quizzical Vneezl posed. "There's no directions, no lines in the sand. no nothing."

"But still we must search," Thaulab said, "Look to the mountains. They also have a significant shape."

Sure enough, the mountains that surrounded the concavity of the town were arrayed in what seemed at first a pair of open hands of six fingers each pointing towards the blue-gray sky. Upon further examination, they just appeared as ragged outcroppings of gray marble. By standing in a certain order within the gazebo, different parts of the range could be seen by the team of adventurers. sometimes a solitary crag was visible, sometimes several pointed toward a specific place within the building. The double shadows of the suns made an interesting pattern upon the floor that perhaps indicated the points on an unseen map.

"We should stay, at least till twilight," Tovalu concluded, "Then we can see what the shadows really mean.

"Then we shall," Oteph said gruffly.

As noon turned to afternoon and afternoon gave way to twilight, the spiders came each one from different regions of the town. Converging on the field in radial formations, they surrounded the gazebo. Their shepherds, the Zepab, also dismounted and sat on the ground in apparent high expectation As the fleeting hours of the day gave way to the bright shining of the asteroid belt and the moon that was in perpetual orbit around the planet, rays of light dashed through the assemblage. The shepherds raised their eyes toward the lights while the spiders seemed to pay silent obeisance to it. The Kweegons and Oteph were dazzled by the shimmering rays and were blinded at first. As their eyes and visual screens filtered out the extreme glare, they could see pathways through the dusty field that ran directly from the center to the town streets beyond. It wasn't long before the visitors were seen by the worshiping shepherds who drew out their slings and blow-pipes at once.

Hard and sharp pebbles glanced off of the hard shell armor that was worn by Tovalu and Vneezl. Meanwhile Thaulab dodged the flying matter with the ease of an acrobat. Oteph had drawn his whip and was twirling it in every direction to avoid being hit. Eventually, he and the team were able to advance a bit and take the offensive against the worshippers who seemed to have a surreal bravery and lack of fear. Oteph's long whip cut gashing holes in the supple skin of the Zepabs that surrounded him while Tovalu and Vneezl had similar luck with their hammers that crushed skulls and broke bodies in half. "t this time, Thaulab stood perfectly still with a troubled look on his face.

"Look. Stop. You are murdering them," he said in a voice that seemed both muted but earth-rending. "Stop at once." He grabbed Oteph's whip by its hilt and quickly stowed it away in his tunic. In a similar way, he grabbed the hammers from the others and let them fall to the ground. Even as he did this, rows and rows of spiders parted and left a large pathway about fifty lengths wide beginning at the gazebo and reaching to the edge of the town. In the air, a soft whisper could be heard along with a slow scraping sound. The sounds of the scraping grew and the whisper grew into a cry like that of an injured animal. Eventually, the team of visitors could see the source of the noise. It was a small brown creature that walked low to the ground on four legs. Twin mandibles were set at the top of the creature's neck and a short spiked tail was raised high over the back of its body. As the creature ambled further, the cry changed to a blood-curdling yell of anger. Behind the creature, on a small sled, a dead creature lay. It was a female Igoilenat. Fair hair adorned the head of the once-lovely woman and a copper colored skin peaked through every rip in her clothing. She wore the adornment of the royal house of Racine and the many-colored tunic was that of a princess. Her legs were long and lean and on her body but her chest had been ripped apart apparently with the end of Oteph's whip which had slashed further and further into the crowd than had the hammers. As the four-legged creature approached the gazebo, the party could see the anger and pain in its eyes as it dragged the lifeless woman

"Stay here," Thaulab said as he stepped off of the gazebo steps toward the small creature. *This creature is psychic, he continued silently*

What is your purpose and where are your pains? he asked. The creature looked puzzled for a moment and the shrieked so loud that the rest of the team was shocked by the shrill sound. The dead woman almost fell off of the sled in the commotion.

The animal asked why it is being killed, Thaulab added.

The team looked down at the creature who suddenly looked weak and helpless. It shivered with apparent fear as it was near the feet of Oteph and the other Kweegons. Oteph grinned at the small creature and offered it his hand to smell.

"Hey there, little fella'," he said, nut the creature just let out a low warning growl and leaped upon him tearing his light armor to shreds in places and flaying his skin in others. The creature looked even more ferocious now that it had Oteph's bright red blood on its mandibles and about its head and neck. But Oteph returned to gaze at the beast and, as he did so, readied his whip. Swinging it high and pulling low until it snapped against the creature's hide, he cut a short gash on the side of the animal's trunk. Just then, Thaulab stood before him. "Stop, I beg of you," he commanded rather than asked. "These people are not yours to have and take advantage of.

"The Hell they aren't." With that, Oteph continued to swing and cut his way through the crowd. He had nearly flayed the small creature to death before it was able to scurry away leaving the dead princess at the feet of the group. As the creature left, the crowd of shepherds and spiders grew to such a frenzied state that one would have thought that they had been directly attacked. Waves upon waves of the spiders and their men converged upon the small group that had killed the princess of the Igoilenat. Oteph and his partners had no choice but to kill everyone who came within their reach. It wasn't remarkably hard to do since the Zepab only wore rags for armor and were mostly barefoot. The fact that they rode without saddles on top of the spiders made them all the more easy to hit and knock down. Oteph used his whip to draw them in while Vneezl and Tovalu chopped and smashed heads with their hammers. Thaulab stood in back of the group with a fretful look on his face constantly fingering the loose ends of his tunic. His face showed shock that changed from anger to hatred and finally disgust. With the strength that only indwells the elderly, he grabbed Oteph and threw him to the ground. He threw down the others afterwards.

"This stops here," he shrieked. He turned his body to the crowd and, sensing that they knew his peaceful nature, let down his guard and sat down among them. The spiders became suddenly docile and ingratiating as he petted their long forelegs and communicated to them silently. He could not speak to the Zepab, but they felt his kindness and sat down with him also. In the distance Oteph and the others looked at the scene in amazement. Thaulab with no armor, no guns and no fear had silently conquered an entire race. Beside themselves, the trio approached the place where Thaulab sat.

"They're as normal as you and I. Just want to find more spacious surroundings. Here's chief Nkuk, their leader. a thin but tall man rose from the group and gave a perfunctory bow followed by a light waggle of the hand. He glared at them.

"Murderers," he growled.

Oteph and Tovalu stood poised in defensive stance. The two looked at the chief in intense hatred and hostility. Oteph fingered the hilt of his flag with his fingertips. Suddenly, the Zepab chief turned back to look at his tribe that sat around him. It was the signal that Oteph was waiting for. In a flash the whip flew from its place and squarely cut into the chief's neck. Angry drops of purple blood spewed from the wound and, as he sunk to the ground he said,

"You. You're the one. You killed her. You killed them."

"Yes and now I do the same to you." With one final blow Oteph severed the chief's head and sent it rolling along the ground towards the open field. "t the barbaric site, the spiders and their riders moved slowly away and filed out of the field with the equal decorum and pomp as they had come in.

Oteph was tired. His right arm ached horribly and his once clean clothes were drenched in the sweat and the blood of the Zepab people. Tovalu and Vneezl looked with puzzlement upon Oteph and his actions, but Thaulab trembled with anger.

"If you had not known the way, fat one, I would have killed you there." Thaulab looked toward the dark sky that had now filled with stars. "look. There she is," he said as he pointed toward a bright light that streaked across the sky, "The Regiceld. and the Hive."

Just as he said the words, Oteph had a vision in his head of the vast mental capacity of the beings that inhabited every corner of the former merchant carrier. Bo'agg and the prison escape and Th'dnuuk and the star port escape. The Hive had been life for him in a life of envy, lust and murder. Thaulab knew what he thought of and the guilt of having to kill both the princess and the chief. Oteph looked out over the dark field that was formerly alive and bustling with the large arachnids. Where did they go , he wondered. Wrapping his flag in tight coils about the handle, he stowed the weapon away and looked toward his compatriots for even a little guidance. Thaulab only looked at him with disgust and the others were likewise disappointed.

"We must go back to the boat," Thaulab finally said. The trip back to the boat took several days over the rocky stones that lay outside the town. The team lay down to rest in various small building until they reached the boat. On the first morning, they awoke to find themselves surrounded by the wondering eyes of a group of Igoilenat.

"Perhaps a family," Thaulab said. The Kweegons then placed their hands on top each creature's head wringing it for information and The party met many such small persons as they traveled. They even met what could have been the broken-down mayor of the town, a short and stout middle-aged man. "bout his shoulders he wore the tattered rags of a once fine robe that bore the purple rosette of the town's seal. By this time, the "mayor" wore only dirt and grime on his head instead of the smart purple cap that indicated authority. Surrounding him on the ground sat a collection of tired old men in similar costumes. " city council.

"So...This is the 'resurrection'," Vneezl snorted, " Funny, I'd hoped for more." "t the sound of his voice, the mayor looked up at the strangely clad visitors. " look of fear swept over his face as Oteph removed his whip and gestured at the man sitting in the dust.

"Come. Show us the entry way to the city. Where are your people?"

The mayor was too frightened to move, petrified by the stony gaze of the space pirate and his crackling whip. Oteph kicked him to his feet and sent him tumbling before them on the grown. The little man gasped in fright and lay on the ground sobbing.

Nineteen

Walking backwards and gesticulating wildly with each new epithet against his racial relations, he brought them to an underground tunnel that led to an enclosed space. On the ground, dirt and grease lay mixed together as though the small lot was once used as a parking bay for a primitive ship or wheeled transport. The guide simply pointed towards a black steel door at the back of the chamber and said, "There, the glory of the Igoilenat. The people you seek." He pounded on the door five times and entered when one of the occupants peered out into the dark chamber. Oteph was the first of the group to bluster through the door and what he saw amazed him. Rows and rows of gaming tables were set up against each side of a massive room filled with people the likes of which he had never seen before. It was clear that they were not Igoilenat. In fact, many were not even humanoid and pushed themselves in carts or slithered along the carpeted floor.

The quartet of travelers stood dumbfounded in the midst of a room of intense activity centered around simple card games that grew more frenzied as time wore on. It was a gambler's outpost, set away from the dangers of the world and all of its inhabitants Oteph was in his natural element here. Striding confidently up to the tables, he checked on the angles, players and dice of every dealer in the place. Finally determined on one seat for the night he plied his trade. In the small hours of the morning, smoldering and smoky air set about the room like a glaze of frost. Oteph had won nearly every bit of small and large money in the place. He shut them down and smiled knowingly back at his friends and his unknown guide. With wads of cash stuffed into his now ragged psi-suit, he made for the door.

"You," he said pointing to one of the other men. "Show the way."

The other, a young-looking man in what appeared to be his twenties, hopped to his feet and gestured back toward the center of the block.

"We're everywhere. Come along." With that the man turned his back on them and started walking in the direction he had indicated.

1"We were the ones we left behind, you know," he said as he shuffled his feet lazily through the powdery dust that seemed to pervade every crack and panel in every build hut and house. And they say that the "Asunur did this to us. We didn't do it. They did. They and their stupid lists. Only the intelligent ones survived."

As the man guided them through the town's alleyways and side streets, he grew angry as he talked about the select few who went underground to hide from the very people

"No time to wait now, we must join our journey once again. In a moment, the [party knew why Oteph was so eager to leave. Three large hairy bipeds had risen from their places at the where Oteph sat and started to silently but purposefully follow him through the room.

"Can ya' believe it?" He said nervously, "They just can't take a joke." Oteph continued to smile and hum to himself as everyone began to notice the small crowd he had attracted. Soon, Oteph and his three enemies had left the game room.

In the darkened filth of the alley way, Oteph could only see his pursuers as large dark monsters. He backed away from them and with his fingers behind his back felt the decayed surface of the wall behind him. His body shook as though he was about to throw up. Out of sheer habit he reached for the place on his belt where he kept his whip. It was gone. Thaulab had taken it. He would die because Thaulab had taken it. Told him to use his mental; prowess rather than his chaotic, berserk style of smashing and decapitating foes. To Thaulab, the flag was uncivilized, brutal and the evident sign of the worst that life can give. Even a Kweegon thought that. These thought whirled through Oteph's head as he found himself beset upon by three of the most horrible creatures he had ever seen. He remembered the lessons of calmness that he had learned while dwelling in the hive. He tried to reach out with his mind, but then was cut off from his thinking by a swift blow by one of the thugs. He barreled through the alley landing in such a way that the full weight of his body caused his head to crash into the brick with such a forced that he burst a small hole in the wall. While he pretended to lay unconscious, he fingered the hole, estimated its size and considered the amount of strength it would take to widen it. Any place was better than outside with these bullies, he thought. Before he could crystallize a new thought of escape, He was picked up and smashed against another portion of the wall, equally as loose. Oteph could feel his teeth loosening, bright red blood began to flow from his mouth. Still, with each blow, he felt more resolved than ever.

"Just try to take me down, you scum, " he growled as angry cat. While the battle wore on, Thaulab and the others exited the casino and looked on their old friend who lay limp as a rag while above him gloated three of the dirtiest creatures that they had seen in the civilized regions. They were the unreadables, beings too simple and straight of thought that they were of little or no psychic value. Thaulab frowned as he grabbed Oteph's old whip from his pack. He balanced it on his tentacled fingers as if to signal Oteph's life hanging in the balance of his fingers.

"Won't you help him," Vneezl pleaded, "Surely now he needs us."

"Hmmm," muttered Thaulab as he straightened the whip and wrapped its fibers firmly against the hilt and then tucked it into his tunic.

"What are you...crazy" Vneezl hissed, "... just leaving him there?"

"No. Not leaving. Educating," Thaulab's stentorian voice echoed loud enough that the three beasts paused to look back at him and his two companions. The pause in the action allowed Oteph the opportunity to slink backwards along the brick wall where he lay bleeding waiting to find a larger gap in the wall. Thaulab gazed at him irritably and with a hand to his forehead began searching through the minds of the thugs. They ceased to be interested in Oteph an instead turned their attention to the tall green aliens that were Oteph's friends. Thaulab quickly plucked Oteph's whip from his tunic and passed it to Tovalu who uncoiled it with a look of admiration.

So this is how the savages did it.

Simple unthinking brutes had obviously cleared the land of the original natives while establishing a code of street law that favored the strong outsiders and crushed the poor and miserable. Tovalu looked

Tovalu spun the long cords above his head and brought them crashing down on the nearest of the creatures. The light blow knock the creature off of its feet. The force of its fall, dazed it for a moment and Tovalu concentrated his gaze on another target, but by the time his throw of the whip was begun, the first grabbed the ends of the cords, not paying attention to the burning of his flesh, and drew Tovalu within arm's length. With a swift, sharp blow, it brought Tovalu to the ground. In the meantime, Oteph had risen halfway to his knees and was searching for a suitable exit. With the flag gone, he had little reason to stay while his friends were battered to pieces. His last view of the scene was that of a fallen Tovalu waving a blood soaked hand and he felt him in his mind,

Stop. Oteph only you can save us now. Please. Oteph continued to make his way through the broken wall only stopping to shake his head sadly at those he left behind

Oteph looked up only to be blinded by bright lights that emanated from a single source on the opposite wall of a chamber that shone directly into the breach in the wall that led into the alley. After some time, Oteph regained his sight and was able to find himself in the middle of a bright auditorium. Rows and rows of hard metal seats converged on a small platform where a lectern and a large heavy table lay set up for use presumably for a speech or lecture. As he made his way down the stairs toward the stage, Oteph noticed a soft shuffle of footsteps that came from the sides and below the auditorium.

Oteph ducked and concealed himself in the midst

Of a row of chairs. As quickly as he had done so, fair-skinned bipeds began pouring into the hall from every entrance. The clattering of footsteps and the squeaking sounds of the metal seats was deafening. As the room became full, Oteph feared for his life and rose to conceal himself behind of a panel of the wall. The people were not Saurians like himself, but their fair skin and light-colored hair made him think more of Xerxus than of Andilax. Oteph had not been so close to his own home in ages. And here they were sitting with pens, papers and folios. After some time, a short man appeared at the lectern. On the top of a head of silvery white hair, he wore a purple miter that delicately adorned the garish features of old age. He momentarily tapped upon the microphone to test the sound quality. Then, in a garbled Andilaxian dialect, he started to read a sheet of paper to the assembly.

"Truly, my brothers, this a bad time. Some say that the invasion has begun, but I say we must fight," he said, "The league of science has reported visual contact with a large host of battle tenders and shuttlecraft in close orbit of this planet. Hive-dwelling creatures, we have decided to call them Kweegons, feast on the mental energies of life-forms above the level of sapience. These creatures these Kweegons I guess they're called, are powerful mind flaying creatures. They will eat us alive if we do not prevent them. The Lord Racine has only allocated enough shields for the protection of a few. And naturally, the increasing population of the Zepab will; not hurt either as they are immune as are their hairy cousins." As the wizened professor spoke, the "students" scribbled in their notes. The meeting went on for hours and, as Oteph concealed himself, he could not prevent the loss of blood from his open wounds from forming a large pool in the center of the carpet where he stood. Soon the stain would betray him to the crowd of apparently well-educated Igoilenat.

Oteph remained as calm as possible behind the screen, but his legs grew tired with standing and he could feel the world beginning to tip and spin around him. He had to bandage his wounds or be discovered or simply die from the loss of his life-sustaining fluids. Just as thought of his plight, a bloody-faced Thaulab stepped silently through the doors of the auditorium. Followed by Vneezl and Tovalu, he placed his hands to his brow and held them there. He was communicating and smiling for the first time in a long while. Oteph felt him searching the minds of each and every individual that sat in the hall. Consequently, the hall grew quiet and the audience slumped forward in their chairs. " white haze settled over the crowd as Thaulab concentrated. . They were all dead and yet, He could still feel their souls wrenching and crying in agony and confusion.

Oteph sensed panic and fear so intense that her believed himself to be witness to the destruction of an entire race.

He lifted his feet from the blood-soaked rug to see that a fine coating of powder was gradually covering the floor and accumulating on the clothes of those who lay unconscious in the audience. The speaker's miter had fallen from his head and was nearly white from the penetration of the powder. In a few moments, Thaulab followed by the rest placed his hands by his sides. Seeking Oteph from behind the screen, Tovalu and Vneezl trudged silently over the ever-increasing white powder.

It is like we had to do. We asked and you said yes, Oteph.

"But you killed all of them. Why?"

Vneezl and Tuvalo simply shrugged their shoulders," because it is what we came to do." Thaulab, too, had a similar sad look about him that implied the immediacy of their deed. "Join with us or be destroyed with the Igoilenat."

"I have nothing to do with this scum," Oteph sputtered, "Their death is my life."

We know. That is why we saved you in the alley.

"You what? You did nothing for me. It was I who discovered them, it was I that routed them. "s for these," he pointed as the contorted figures covered in white, "I was well in control."

"No." Thaulab's voice was as sad as it was final. He voiced at Oteph only to show him who was in control, "You did not. Here you are bleeding to death and nearly fainting for lack of food or rest."

It was true. Oteph swayed helplessly against his own weight and the loss of blood and his body feinted for lack of food. "Okay. I am no child. Give me that flag of mine. You don't know how to use it and its lack would be the death of me.

Thaulab snickered throatily as he looked at the short and stout pirate. He haltingly reached for the flag that he had tucked deep within the folds of his tunic and brought it out putting the coiled hilt on Oteph's shoulder. Oteph snatched the whip as soon as he saw it coming towards him. Thaulab looked surprised.

Foolish One. Never do you learn to use your mind rather than this barbaric thong.

"But never do you learn to fight like a man," Oteph was full of his usual bluster as he talked of his own virility, "You don't know the satisfaction of victory, just the assimilation of it."

The Asunur had full control over the Kweegons every time they came into contact with them. Tovalu had never recovered from his first run in with the hardy nomads. His arms and legs still ached from deep scars and lacerations that even months inside the Hive could not fix.

Twenty

The tribes and the Igoilenat settled on a tentative peace, each fearing the agitation and rebellion of the other. The planetary congress reconvened after a long period of peaceful integration with the tribes of the badlands. They were a minority on their own home, but they held out hope by studying all the ancient scripts they could find. Computer networks had sometimes needed to be reconnected and sometimes, totally changed. It took all of the effort of the scientific community to rebuild what was lost and all of the statesmanship of a tyrant to quell the unrest of a skittish public.

The artificial rendering of Lord Racine's voice could be heard as it crackled through primitive audio encoders left over from the old times. His voice was the same everyday as if it were recorded.

Protect your interests in the years ahead as I shall do for mine. Gather your children;

make them safe and pray to God that he might heal us from the affliction."

"Greetings, one and all. As you know," each speech would begin, "We face dire problems in of our land." It was the same year old message that had been fed through the public media avenues for months. Eventually, the people learned to reject the babble and accept the fact that the government as they knew it was probably dead. The time of the Igoilenat was quickly nearing its end without a rescue or savior anywhere in sight. Oteph, too, lost sight of the Igoilenat and chose instead to ally himself with the wilderness tribes of the wastelands the first of which was the Iraarku. The newly adopted Ukkmadaku sought the

The Iraarku hunted with Ukkmadaku at the lead, the never-ending supply of cultural artifacts from the once great civilization. The new leaders of the abandoned museums displayed that which was artistic, scientific and even warlike. Ukkmadaku was the first to strip down the contents of the libraries of war. Gaining higher technology in the means to conquer and enslave was the end that he hoped to reach through the study of the weapons of the Igoilenat. Present in the case and then confiscated were small guns, razor sharp knives and razor wire garrotes. He was in heaven and the troop, dismounted from their spiders, smiled in wonderment at the sight Time never slowed for the tribe as they studied the ancient ways and became accustomed to maritime rather than desert climate. Artifacts such as the pressure gun were copied and then made from wood leather and stone and then given to the tribe's chiefs. The Iraarku grew in military might and sheer territory that they continually had contact with other tribes and the political machine of the Igoilenat. Lord Racine, now a tottering old man leaned on his cane every afternoon as he watched legion s of spiders pass by Capitol every morning, noon and night.

The spiders were difficult to ride. the eight legs nimbly coursed over thick layers of sand while the body swayed and kerthumped against the saddle and riding tackle. Ukkmadaku was about to retire one day from soreness as saw the Nexus, a new outpost for the Iraarku. He would have to stop, rebalance his load and move on to city center where the rest of the tribe waited for him to be enlisted as their chieftain.

His spider already bedecked in the purple of a beadle of the court, but to fit amongst the Paige of the court, he must earn the red colors of high class, the most sought after color of the world that then was. The ceremony was remarkably short, it consisting of a simple changing of garments on his body and on the tackle of the spider. He felt no different than he did as a prisoner or as a member of

Thaulab's ever-renewing Hive. As Oteph, life had consisted of combining a series of selfish conceited acts and calling them, in total, a life of piracy and freedom. The Iraarku did not accept him as such. As a properly graduated spear man, he had learned the ways of a proud man energized by wit and good will. Things totally nauseating had become to him a new life and Yet, as a Saurian, Home was not his land and he missed his beloved Saurians dearly.

The spider-killers came from the south and invaded the land.

And all this when Ukkmadaku was just hitting his stride preparing to lead the main flock for yet another meeting with Princess in the field of the Capitol. The spider-killers traveled on seven legs and bared sharp pinching teeth that were able to rip and tear their way through the a spider's carapace. Ukkmadaku rode his spider proudly in front of the long lines and sections of tribes. He felt a sharp burning sensation as a spider-killer pounced on his mount and set about quickly to dispatch it. Ukkmadaku was thrown far from the fray of clashing claws and the sharp hollow sound of shell against shell. The spider-killers were much like their six legged friends except for the fact that normal bipeds could not ride them. Their spines were covered from front to back with razor-sharp plating and the one place where a mount could be fastened was so far atop the animal's main center of gravity, that to have a rider there would mean a bumpy ride at the least and a horrible fall at the most.

The killers had ten legs: four legs to support a great ovoid body that was protected by a large red carapace and six more to support an extremely flexible middle that came to support a head of sorts with ten eyes, glands for smelling and three antennae to ward off the approach of enemies. The great ant-like creatures wore extremely powerful, sharp claws supported by "Arms" as strong as the purest iridium. If they were not so hated, they would be a marvel to modern natural science. As Ukkmadaku lay bleeding, he watched as his spider was systematically destroyed by the ten-legged beast. Not wishing to provide the next tasty bit to the meal.

Ukkmadaku managed to get inside the sandy entrance to an abandoned pharmacy. There he stayed until his former property was flayed crunched and eaten. The only problem was that the spider-killers came back in greater numbers. They had found his people's den, the secret dwelling of the Iraarku.

He held up a dark hand and waved for the crowd to quiet and the entire crowd was silent for eight hours until the Princess came. As usual, a nexus of pure energy effused the gazebo, and spiders shone gloriously as they filed one-by-one past the personage of the mysterious queen. While Ukkmadaku stood closest to Princess, he drew near to her light and tried to get a closer look at the light that emanated from the folds of her garments. He reached out to touch her and was at the same time severely burned and enlightened. Finally, he realized the meaning behind the nightly visits and why they had come to the habitable regions of Home.

The spiders, their riders and even the opposing tribes converged upon Princess at least once a week. While Ukkmadaku stood in the shining light, he saw the universe as it once was. Ng was a partner star to Home while Andilaxus, Saurus and the remaining stars twirled overhead never meeting and yet seeming to dance with each other. He saw his ancestral home, the filthy corridors of a rock mine. His mother was a miner and his father was a brigand farmer of good reputation. He smiled and supposed that was where he had gained his lust for food, power and money. It all seemed so foolish now. The ignominy of his youth as a petty thief and ignominious farmer seemed far away as he soaked in the light. He felt his spine going stiff and his legs, alive with fire. Suddenly he was home. The sun-bleached soil of Saurus soon enveloped him and he smelled the familiar air and felt the gentle soil of his youth under his thick combat boots.

The spider-killers came from the south and invaded the land. And all this when Ukkmadaku was just hitting his stride preparing to lead the main flock for yet another meeting with Princess in the field of the Capitol. The spider-killers traveled on legs and bared sharp pinching teeth that were able to rip and tear their way through the a spider's carapace. Ukkmadaku rode his spider proudly in front of the long lines and sections of tribes. He felt a sharp burning sensation as a spider-killer pounced on his mount and set about quickly to dispatch it. Ukkmadaku was thrown far from the fray of clashing claws and the sharp hollow sound of shell against shell. The spider-killers were much like their six legged friends except for the fact that normal bipeds could not ride them. Their spines were covered from front to back with razor-sharp plating and the one place where a mount could be fastened was so far atop the animal's main center of gravity, that to have a rider there would mean a bumpy ride at the least and a horrible fall at the most.

The killers had ten legs: four legs to support a great ovoid body that was protected by a large red carapace and six more to support an extremely flexible middle that came to support a head of sorts with ten eyes, glands for smelling and three antennae to ward off the approach of enemies. The great ant-like creatures wore extremely powerful and sharp claws supported by "arms" as strong as the strongest metal. If they were not so hated, they would be a marvel to modern natural science. As Ukkmadaku lay bleeding, he watched as his spider was systematically destroyed by the huge beast. Not wishing to provide the next tasty bit to the meal.

Ukkmadaku managed to get inside the sandy entrance to an abandoned pharmacy. There he stayed until his former property was flayed crunched and eaten. The only problem was that the spider-killers came back in greater numbers. They had found them, the secret place of the Iraarku

He held up a dark hand and waved for the crowd to quiet and the entire crowd was silent for eight hours until the Princess came. As usual, a nexus of pure energy effused the gazebo, an spiders shone gloriously as they filed one-by-one past the personage of the mysterious queen. While Ukkmadaku stood closest to Princess, he drew near to her light and tried to get a closer look at the light that emanated from the folds of her garments. He reached out to touch her and was at the same time severely burned and enlightened. Finally, he realized the meaning behind the nightly visits and why they had come to the habitable regions of Home.

The spiders, their riders and even the opposing tribes converged upon Princess at least once a week. While Ukkmadaku stood in the shining light, he saw the universe as it once was. Ng was a partner star to Home while Andilaxus, Saurus and the remaining stars twirled overhead never meeting and yet seeming to dance with each other. He saw his ancestral home, the filthy corridors of a rock mine. His mother was a miner and his father was a brigand farmer of good reputation. He smiled and supposed that was where he had gained his lust for food, power and money. It all seemed so foolish now. The ignominy of his youth as a petty thief and ignominious farmer seemed far away as he soaked in the light. He felt his spine going stiff and his legs, alive with fire. Suddenly he was home. The sun-bleached soil of Saurus soon enveloped him and he smelled the familiar air and felt the gentle soil of his youth under his thick combat boots.

The spider-killers came from the south and invaded the land. And all this when Ukkmadaku was just hitting his stride preparing to lead the main flock for yet another meeting with Princess in the field of the Capitol. The spider-killers traveled on seven legs and bared sharp pinching teeth that were able to rip and tear their way through the a spider's carapace. Ukkmadaku rode his spider proudly in front of the long lines and sections of tribes. He felt a sharp burning sensation as a spider-killer pounced on his mount and set about quickly to dispatch it. Ukkmadaku was thrown far from the fray of clashing claws and the sharp hollow sound of shell against shell. The spider-killers were much like their six legged friends except for the fact that normal bipeds could not ride them. Their spines were covered from front to back with razor-sharp plating and the one place where a mount could be fastened was so far atop the animal's main center of gravity, that to have a rider there would mean a bumpy ride at the least and a horrible fall at the most.

The spider-killers had ten legs: four legs to support a great ovoid body that was protected by a large red carapace and six more to support an extremely flexible middle that came to support a head of sorts with ten eyes, glands for smelling and three antennae to ward off the approach of enemies. The great ant-like creatures wore extremely powerful and sharp claws supported by arms as strong as the strongest metal. If they were not so hated, they would be a marvel to modern natural science. As Ukkmadaku lay bleeding, he watched as his spider was systematically destroyed and eaten by the huge beast.

Not wishing to provide the next tasty bit to the meal, Ukkmadaku managed to get inside the sandy entrance to an abandoned pharmacy. There he stayed until his former property was flayed crunched and eaten. The only problem was that the spider-killers came back in greater numbers. They had found their den, the secret dwelling of the Iraarku. They were not safe at home and Ukkmadaku realized it

He held up a dark hand and waved for the crowd to quiet and the entire crowd was silent for eight hours until the Princess came. As usual, a nexus of pure energy effused the gazebo, and the spiders shone gloriously as they filed one-by-one past the personage of the mysterious queen. While Ukkmadaku stood closest to Princess, he drew near to her light and tried to get a closer look at the light that emanated from the folds of her garments. He reached out to touch her and was at the same time severely burned and enlightened. Finally, he realized the meaning behind the nightly visits and why they had come to the habitable regions of Home. The glory of the Princess was nearly too much for him. He could not understand it

The spiders, their riders and even the opposing tribes converged upon the Princess at least once a week. While Ukkmadaku stood in the shining light, he saw the universe as it once was. Ng was a partner star to Home while Andilaxus, Saurus and the remaining stars twirled overhead never meeting and yet seeming to dance with each other. He saw his ancestral home, the filthy corridors of a rock mine. His mother was a miner and his father was a brigand farmer of good reputation. He smiled and supposed that was where he had gained his lust for food, power and money. It all seemed so foolish now. The ignominy of his youth as a petty thief and ignominious farmer seemed far away as he soaked in the light. He felt his spine going stiff and his legs, alive with fire. The light surrounded him; burned him.

Suddenly he was home. The Iraarku were but a memory as was the tragedy of the Igoilenat. Oteph knew where he was and he was happy for it.

He didn't know why or how, but he was home: here on Saurus where the temperature was stifling and the soil as hard a metal. The bright sun bleached and baked the barren landscape outside of a hometown that he knew well. The low clay huts were crafted to dissipate intense temperatures of the failing sun. He that was Ukkmadaku was now Oteph again. He had crossed the nexus from one life to another, but now he was home. What a relief, he thought, I wonder if they'll kill me.

Worshipping the sun, Oteph slid down into the warm dust that covered the side of a road that led to town. The heat surrounded him like a blanket and he embraced the soil that he had once tilled for the life of his family. That was before the visitors: before the ravaging ones. Oteph's dreams were troubled with the memories of the old days. He had sworn himself to the life of a bandit if, for no other reason, that he could avenge his brothers against

Twenty one

His body hovered as it were by the unseen influence of a spirit over the environs of his youth. Oteph saw his father and father and brothers killed by a man with a heavy iron awl that seemed to sever their bodies into quarters. He stood gazing from a corner as his family bled to death crying out for his help. He saw how an unconcerned youth regarded the bleeding deaths and callously searched their bodies for money and gold. This young Oteph listened to the pleas of his brothers as they lay in death. Oteph frowned and looked toward the door. The murderer must have left with something. He must have. The small Saurian sun blazed heavily upon the small soil huts of Innaebrius and Oteph glared through the brightness, he saw the bright speck of a shuttle hurtling through the sky and seeming, as it were, to be challenging the very atmosphere of Saurus itself. What could he have taken, Oteph wondered aloud to himself. His family was poor. His father only earned the title of Star Master in his advancing age and his brothers had long ago dedicated their lives to farming, fornication and robbery, the three joys of planetary life. It was then that Oteph returned to his family's hut, retrieved the quickly deteriorating bodies and buried them deep beneath the black soil.

Fortreus' girls would doubtless come for him as would the small cadre of females that orbited the beastly passions of Porphry his elder brother. Now that they lay in state in the fertile soil that they once loved, his noble rakish family would be in his hands alone. Soon, his shoulders held the dutiful teary-eyed faces of women that professed their loved yet once more. Oteph stood and wondered at the sight. Would maidens have ever sought him out had he died in such violence? The answer was unclear to him and bye and bye he let the young women go away to newer times with fresher men.

Oteph could see himself over the following years growing into himself. He held no more love for Saurus and began to hate even the substance of the soil that gave him his life and identity to everyone who lived there. Confounded by his brothers' deaths he left the land of his kin and joined with bands of outsiders. "t first, the small raids chafed against his nature. He raped, abused and killed most of those he met thinking all the while of that bloody axe that had robbed him of direction in life and the emptiness he felt as the community grieved for them and not him. Oteph became angry and disconsolate. He frequented the shady dives of the town while drowning his troubles in sex, drugs and eating. Soon he grew as his ego twice the size of one man. He was no longer a sexual prize to women he met, but a short force whip made that unimportant applying a constant stream of electricity to the flesh would produce immediate compliance. Oteph had soiled his spirit with the lives of others and now he turned to himself.

Oteph saw himself floating the dream as he had floated through life. Never reaching the rank of a star master, he flounced around center street and made a life of thievery and general rapaciousness, but the life produced a dull ache within him. He hated Saurus and had used up all friendship and trust that he had earned as a farmer. Everyone knew his "game." That is, everyone except him. He was lost. He learned to trust a flash of his force whip to any man or woman. In the days, he felt ennui and in the night he choked up what he thought was his own blood, his own life slipping away from him. He joined the spice freighter Freiheit and began a career among the stars. Working in the galley most days, he fraternized with the crew, but soon became known for his unbalanced nature and natural hatred for hand-held weapons especially crushing and impaling instruments.

The off-watches were hated times for Oteph as he strove to suppress his dislike for everyone. Carrying the force whip was too great a temptation so he had the captain stow it in the lowest berth of the ship. Only then could he concentrate on his cooking that afforded him no small amount of notoriety among the crew. Years of work on the freight lines did not mellow his anger towards Saurus, but he grew placid with his regular station in life and his fingers found other things besides weapons to hold. He was almost free.

Stalsius Frink, first prince of the Rushtan royal dynasty arrived as a passenger at the star port at Ng and, wishing passage back to Saurus, was given a primary cabin aboard the freighter. Stalsius' cock-sure gait and loud flamboyant demeanor turned Oteph purple with rage. Such behavior didn't belong on any ship as far as he was concerned. He could see the evidence of the sheltered royal life on Stalsius in the way he moved gracefully down the corridors. Always dressed in the light purple robes of the king, Stalsius knew he was a hot item and held his head high as though his very presence was a gift that he alone could give. Oteph had long ago developed the plain style of the workman-farmer, but Stalsius dressed himself with ribbons and lace and minced down the corridors as though he was a living flower. Oteph feared him. He knew that his conduct aboard ship would be made known to his new guest and he feared for what threads of respect that he still possessed.

"It's all right, man," Stalsius would usually say, "You're just too bugged out. Don't think so much." Oteph wondered at the speech of his long-past friend. Later, Oteph would curl up behind the waste units and weep softly until sleep overtook him or until other officers used the room. He was as guilty as sin and he knew it and he knew that Stalsius knew. In the future, Oteph confined his wanderings to the inner chambers of the galley where he cooked bland, unsalted food for months until the Freiheit reached the port at Saurus.

Presumably, Stalsius left the ship to return to his wealthy following. "t least that was what Oteph hoped. Instead, becoming thrilled and enchanted by the Freiheit, he returned bringing his family and retinue with him. Oteph, sure of himself, once again, proudly wore his force whip as he paced up and down the main corridors. It was refreshing to own the halls again and his whip gave him the assurance he needed to move forward.

"Now, there's a funny tool for a cook," he heard a familiar voice say. Before he could think properly, he felt the cold hand of Stalsius Frink on his neck. Instinctively reaching for his whip, Oteph whirled around and faced the surprised royal who had obviously meant only playfulness in the gesture. The problem with Stalsius, Oteph thought, was just that he flounced around too much; prancing down corridors that were reserved for sober-minded technicians and engineers. Oteph was surprised by his following. Stalsius developed friends and paramours . Oteph hated him for this. He might have entertained lofty feelings from time to time, but in the end, he was just a pair of dirty hands, a flat-footed, lumpy, foul-smelling landsman. The feelings confounded him just as his brothers females had done before. He was lost. Months aboard the ship did nothing to comfort Oteph. In his past were so many lies and secrets and all the while, complete strangers treated him as just another innocent space hand. But he was not innocent. He sought every moment to find his brother's killers. Every moment he stood alone he thought of it. Hateful thoughts invaded his reveries and countenance darkened just as his habits of washing and cleansing. Oteph saw Stalsius almost once a day while he traveled from the crew bunks toward the galley. He watched his mincing steps and animated hands and fingers with sheer disgust. Why he couldn't be like others was beyond him. But Stalsius liked Oteph. He rose to greet him each time the self-proclaimed lumpy farmer emerged from the place of eating.

"Hail, friend," he would say, " How goes the night? I like those boots." Oteph felt increasingly uncomfortable around Stalsius. Boots were boots, hands were hands and a dirty greasy tunic was his daily wardrobe. Oteph sought to avoid him at all costs. Lingering long in the crew quarters did not work because the traveling coterie of royals roamed the hallways and alleys almost constantly and prince Stalsius was no better. His natural curiosity towards all things pertaining to star travel had him up and peeking into every nook and cranny of the relatively small freighter. Oteph tried wearing filthy clothes, smearing his face with grease and kitchen filth, but even that did not help.

"Hell-ooo, Oteph, My, you must be working hard this morning. I admire that." Oteph felt that he would soon throw up. "I like a hard working man."

"Why don't you leave me alone," Oteph growled under his breath, "I hate you."

Stalsius seemed to stop in mid-step, his eyes and face suddenly robbed of their usual joy and zest. "Oh, well, It can't be that bad, can it?"

"Yes it can-and it is," Oteph said, "I must do my job and you must do yours. I'm sorry if I hurt your feelings." The pair slowly turned away from each other and as Oteph slunk down the corridor to the galley, Stalsius stood still as though he were attached to the floor. Eventually, he turned from the scene and strode toward the luxury cabins, his long purple cloak drifting in stately fashion along the ground. Though he walked and held the affectations of a prince, Stalsius felt for the first time like a spider that had been stepped. " bug squashed by a piece of hard wood or as a drifting mass of scum in a horrid swamp. He hated himself. Thrice had he entrusted himself to people he cared about and now, with Oteph angered, thrice had he been beaten back on the chin. Stalsius remained in his quarters.

***

Oteph had raped, pillaged, burned robbed and blackmailed, but he never had killed one of his own. The feeling was horrible. With some thoughtless and snide comments, he had beaten down the character of an innocent, weak and unsure fellow traveler. Royals always were delicate and this he knew well, but Stalsius was different. With unmitigated trust, the young prince would have given him a new life He held his body tightly against the wall to prevent a complete collapse and then made his way to the refuse units where he remained for hours rocking and weeping and clenching.

In Oteph's tortured young mind, he saw the waste of life that he had created because just as he was sitting and rocking in the lavatory, Stal7sius the prince was languishing in despair also. The velvet-covered walls of the first class cabin seemed to be constricting his ability to breathe. He felt as if the weight of the ship had come to rest on the top of his chest and that the doom of his life had finally caught up with him

Stalsius, for his own part, remained sequestered away and ceased wearing his peculiar robes and instead dressed shabbily in a used leather doublet that he had found among his more unwholesome things. He no longer showered, shaved or revitalized the pores of his skin. He wore the slippers of penury instead of his fine black boots that clicked affirmatively each time he took a step. As for Oteph, soon things were back to normal. Sloppiness was his normality and an ignominious attitude his frequent friend.

Oteph focused his days and sleeping periods to the creation of new food dishes and dainty deserts that became the staple of the royal contingent aboard ship. Soon, he was known as "the king of fluff" an d "Lord lard bucket." None of it really bothered him until one day he saw the downtrodden Stalsius slinking through the double doors of the galley and taking a seat by himself at a table usually set aside for the plebeian ensigns or low class travelers. Taking note of his presence for only a moment, Oteph kept ladling up a sloppy gruel to a sudden influx of crew and general persons. One by one, the tables filled up and finally, the table where Stalsius sat in lonely and excruciating languor. He panicked. Having no food and no one to establish his presence, he was utterly alone. Standing up from the table, he backed into another crewmember.

"Outta my way, pantywaist," grumbled a soldier. Stalsius lurched one way and then another to avoid the growing crowd of ship hands. He was afraid and as he backed further into the crowd, he found himself panicking again and the world about His retreat led him all the way back into the heated serving area where Oteph stood, mindlessly slopping away with his military regulation spoon and oversized yellow spatula. " greasy brown apron was strapped across his chest and flowed down toward his waist.

Twenty two

"You," he said pointing to one of the other men. "Show the way."

The other,. a young-looking man in what appeared to be his twenties, hopped to his feet and gestured back toward the center of the block.

"We're everywhere. Come along." With that the man turned his back on them and started walking in the direction he had indicated.

"We were the ones we left behind, you know," he said as he shuffled his feet lazily through the powdery dust that seemed to pervade every crack and panel in every building and small hut and house. "And they say that the Asunur did this to us. We didn't do it. They did. The high council. They and their stupid lists. Only the intelligent ones survived."

As the man guided them through the town's alleyways and side streets, he grew angry as he talked about the select few who went underground to hide from the very people who naturally lived   there.

"No time to wait now, we must join our journey once again. In a moment, the [party knew why Oteph was so eager to leave. Three large hairy bipeds had risen from their places at the where Oteph sat and started to silently but purposefully follow him through the room.

"Can ya' believe it?" He said nervously, "They just can't take a joke." Oteph continued to smile and hum to himself as everyone began to notice the small crowd he had attracted. Soon, Oteph and his three enemies had left the game room.

Twenty three

, look who crawled out of a rat-hole, It's prince what's-his-name." Stalsius wore an expression of deep shock as he saw and heard from a man that he had once admired.

"Yeah, that's me."

Stalsius trembled and felt his face burn with embarrassment as he stood before Oteph and the ever-increasing line of hungry crew. Oteph paused in mid-slop and looked carefully at the prince. Oteph who was his friend seemed different somehow.

"You better get some food; you look tired. Get it from Wendy."

Wendy was the cook's second mate and, unlike her senior, was always cleanly dressed. Pots, pans and plates as well as silver and utensils had their place and were neatly arranged around a spotless work area. Stalsius thought it was the result of a lifetime of serving up mayonnaise and white sauce, but it was just her way. Soon he had been given enough food to last a few more days or perhaps a week if he was careful.

"Be sure and come back," Oteph called after him, "The guys all miss you." Oteph knew his comment was untrue and yet to him the power of the snide remark was so deeply ingrained that he felt he couldn't do anything but say things that were meant to hurt. He might just as well have said: "Relieve us, mighty prince, your presence is too potent for us."

Stalsius stumbled out the double doors laced his doublet and tied it straight an then made a slow deliberate return to his quarters. That night he gorged on the food he had gotten and with a full stomach he began to tend to his hygiene .

Oteph saw himself staying aboard the Freiheit for a year, the time it took to travel from the royal outpost on Ng to the low-tech world of Saurus. Space flight was not without excitement, though. While crossing the nexus, the Freiheit was for a short time captured and pillaged by pirates. Oteph, as cook, had little to do with any of it until the boarding party desired to relieve the galley of its fresh water and food supply. During a regular mealtime session when Oteph served as swiftly as a high-speed robot, the attacks came. First, the galley was flooded with light and under the brightness slipped a dozen men all armed to the teeth with concussion helmets, distraction rays and small brass knives. The crew were taken aback for a moment as they observed the scene. Oteph, himself, stopped serving, dropped his spoon and spatula and drew his force whip, but there was little he could do as the invaders soon overpowered the unarmed diners. Seeing a gap in the light, Oteph walked towards the corridor where he saw Stalsius ambling down to the galley in his usual tentative, tenuous manner.

"Get down, prince," he yelled, but Stalsius only paused to look about him and, seeing nothing, continued on his slow, dejected and unmusical way. Oteph was horrified to see an attacker creep up beside the prince and slide a long silver blade into Stalsius' cotton doublet and flowing blouse.

'No! Stop," Oteph shouted. But he was too late. The invader had wounded the prince seriously and as Stalsius slumped to the floor, Oteph was filled with rage. Placing his fingers on the bloodied shirt and the flowing wound beneath it, Oteph held Stalsius in his arms

"Say not that you have fallen." In the sequenced images, Oteph couldn't believe his eyes as he saw his dream self helping the shrinking violet of a man. Stalsius looked equally surprised. The formerly brutish cook had turned soft at the sight of his misfortune. Stalsius' body grew limp as he feinted for loss of blood. After carrying Stalsius to the medical bay, Oteph applied a stimp pack to the gaping wound, wiped his own fingers of the prince' bright red blood and returned to the corridors where a much larger conflict had ensued, Regularly employed security and planet troops fought a losing battle against the much better armed invaders. The situation was hopeless, but Oteph drew on his natural meanness for a solution. With the force whip in one hand and his other stretched out to balance his ungainly body, he went on the attack. The force whip could bind, wound or even lacerate foes depending on its aspect and usage. Oteph was able to bind and shock up to two troopers at one time.

"long, heated boredom engulfed the small freighter as the regular spacers tried desperately to regain control over the Freiheit and expel the pirates. Oteph had long since left the galley and had taken up a strategic position amidships where his large round body rested against the forward pylon of the medical bay where Stalsius still lay, weak and delirious from the wound that had only just started to open again.

Oteph smartly kept an eagle's gaze over the medical bay as he sought, now from long distance to wound or render impotent the invaders. But now the tide had begun to turn. The crew had dropped their meals rushed back to their stations and, with the help of the formerly languid royal retinue, had begun to beat the unwelcome guests back to the airlock. Oteph wondered at the unexpected usefulness of the royals who, at the sight of danger, he expected that they would shed their colored robes and flee. Instead, the incredibly fierce group and produced thin sharp blades that were identical in size and shape but used by them became deadly. Could Stalsius be one of these royal heroes, he thought to himself. One look back to the place where he came and he panicked. Stalsius had slipped away again.

Oteph had always seen royals the way that the rest of the world saw them, as weakened, dainty, girlish men and self-important ladies, but the incident on the Freiheit did much to change his thinking. Underneath their silken robes and within their festive royal array, they carried the skill of expert soldiers. With knives as small as fresh sprout of a tree branch, they could overpower the attack of a massive brutish villain. Oteph, watching from the safety of the medical bay watched as the princes and ladies slowly took the battle away from the pirates by luring them back into the bridge past the stateroom. Slowly, one by one, the future leaders of Saurus moved silently from their chambers amidships. Fully trained in courtly battle, such royals rarely had the need to use them in real life. But this day was somehow different. It was surreal and yet it felt nice to them. The royal travelers moved quietly and with daggers made of gold awaited their prey. Courtly battle the computer, engineering and console controls. The royals slipped back to their rooms as quietly as they had come forth, most of them showing little signs of exercise.

Oteph turned to face Stalsius as he lay unconscious on the table. With what little medical knowledge he had, Oteph rifled through the cupboards and containers desperately searching for something to stanch the bleeding. Unsuccessfully, he only wound up making a mess of a formerly tidy room. Just then, captain Wiggins, commander of the health and well-being unit arrived to find the embarrassed, fearful Oteph holding handfuls of medical dressings from small gauze strips to instant heat packs. "t the sight of the Captain, he dropped everything on the floor.

"What are you doing to this prince?" He demanded. "I'm calling security."

"This man needs several stimp packs, but I can't find them," Oteph protested.

"He needs that, it's true, but you need out of here." It did not take long for the keenly dressed security patrol to appear at the door of the medical bay.

"Take this savage out of here and don't let him loose again. He has killed our great prince." The men strong-armed Oteph into a pair of strong binders and forced him to leave the room.

"He needs medicine. I can help," Oteph yelled back towards the medical bay.

The medical captain cursed to himself as he looked down at Stalsius who had now drawn close to the very threshold of death.

"How do pigs like that ever get aboard," he muttered, "Oh, well you wouldn't know."

Oteph was held in confinement for the rest of the journey. Branded as a thief and murderer, he was banished from Saurus and remained aboard the Freiheit only as long as he could find a system that could excuse his criminal past. But the time aboard the Freiheit changed him. With Stalsius as a friend, he had the chance of a new life as an acceptable, healthy member of the society of space. As a murderer, his was a life that was once again cursed to being planet bound on a remote system with little or no civilized society. He soon forgot the ways of the gentry making himself content to lay in wait for yet another foray among society. After all, here on a new system no one cared about royalty because there was none. Saurus was primitive, backward and at the same time unhealthy. Oteph began a new life quickly. The rudimentary star port on the planet where he lived was only serviceable to small pods and the all terrain vehicles that they carried. Getting aboard would not be easy. Oteph still carried the force whip that had saved him from many troubles in the past, but somehow his strength failed him. The royal folk were a people more gentle and timid than anyone or anything he had ever seen, but when provoked they were silent an deadly warriors. This appealed to Oteph and he thought of it each time he coiled up the 6 foot whip and replaced it at his side. To pick a fight was easy. To enjoin quietness was something he knew nothing about.

Oteph suddenly awoke to the feeling of a sharp boot slamming against his side. It seemed like days had passed since he fell asleep Under the overhang. What little shadows there were did not protect him from the afternoon rays of the bright sun. His skin ached from severe burns and blisters welled up on the tender skin of his face. As his eyes adjusted to the bright light he saw a huge personage towering above him. To his amazement, the person wore the lavender of Saurus and the broach of the king binding her cloak around herself. It was a princess of the realm.

"Stalsius said I might find you here," she said in a voice that was barely discernible from the warm wind, "I had my chance to kill you and I could have done so easily."

Oteph, parched from the extreme heat and lack of heat was speechless. " princess on a forbidden planet, he wondered.

"You must be far from home," He gasped, "Who came with you to keep you safe?"

"No one. I trust not in the affairs of men and machines."

The woman stepped back a few paces until she stood in the direct sunlight. The light shimmered as it hit her broach and the wind blew through her hair creating a rippling effect that was not unlike the waves of an ocean. But what ocean was this, he wondered. Her flowing lavender robe brushed against the hot stones

"Take me with you," Oteph said as he struggled to his feet, arms and legs aching from the run-in with the spiders.

Twenty four

"Hail, friend," he would say, "How goes the night? I like those boots." Oteph felt increasingly uncomfortable around Stalsius. Boots were boots, hands were hands and a dirty greasy tunic was his daily wardrobe. Oteph sought to avoid him at all costs. Lingering long in the crew quarters did not work because the traveling coterie of royals roamed the hallways and alleys almost constantly and prince Stalsius was no better. His natural curiosity towards all things pertaining to star travel had him up and peeking into every nook and cranny of the relatively small freighter. Oteph tried wearing filthy clothes, smearing his face with grease and kitchen filth, but even that did not help.

"Hell-ooo, Oteph, My, you must be working hard this morning. I admire that." Oteph felt that he would soon throw up. "I like a hard working man."

"Why don't you leave me alone," Oteph growled under his breath, "I hate you."

Stalsius seemed to stop in mid-step, his eyes and face suddenly robbed of their usual joy and zest. "Oh, well, It can't be that bad, can it?"

"Yes it can-and it is," Oteph said, "I must do my job and you must do yours. I'm sorry if I hurt your feelings." The pair slowly turned away from each other and as Oteph slunk down the corridor to the galley, Stalsius stood still as though he were attached to the floor. Eventually, he turned from the scene and strode toward the luxury cabins, his long purple cloak drifting in stately fashion along the ground. Though he walked and held the affectations of a prince, Stalsius felt for the first time like a spider that had been stepped. " bug squashed by a piece of hard wood or as a drifting mass of scum in a horrid swamp. He hated himself. Thrice had he entrusted himself to people he cared about and now, with Oteph angered, thrice had he been beaten back on the chin. Stalsius remained in his quarters.

***

Oteph had raped, pillaged, burned robbed and blackmailed, but he never had killed one of his own. The feeling was horrible. With some thoughtless and snide comments, he had beaten down the character of an innocent, weak and unsure fellow traveler. Royals always were delicate and this he knew well, but Stalsius was different. With unmitigated trust, the young prince would have given him a new life. He held his body tightly against the wall to prevent a complete collapse and then made his way to the refuse units where he remained for hours rocking and weeping and clenching.

In Oteph's tortured young mind, he saw the waste of life that he had created because just as he was sitting and rocking in the lavatory, Stalsius the prince was languishing in despair also. The velvet-covered walls of the first class cabin seemed to be constricting his ability to breathe. He felt as if the weight of the ship had come to rest on the top of his chest and that the doom of his life had finally caught up with him

Stalsius, for his own part, remained sequestered away and ceased wearing his peculiar robes and instead dressed shabbily in a used leather doublet that he had found among his more unwholesome things. He no longer showered, shaved or revitalized the pores of his skin. He wore the slippers of penury instead of his fine black boots that clicked affirmatively each time he took a step. As for Oteph, soon things were back to normal. Sloppiness was his normality and an ignominious attitude his frequent friend.

Oteph focused his days and sleeping periods to the creation of new food dishes and dainty deserts that became the staple of the royal contingent aboard ship. Soon, he was known as "the king of fluff" an d "Lord lard bucket." None of it really bothered him until one day he saw the downtrodden Stalsius slinking through the double doors of the galley and taking a seat by himself at a table usually set aside for the plebeian ensigns or low class travelers. Taking note of his presence for only a moment, Oteph kept ladling up a sloppy gruel to a sudden influx of crew and general persons. One by one, the tables filled up and finally, the table where Stalsius sat in lonely and excruciating languor. He panicked. Having no food and no one to establish his presence, he was utterly alone. Standing up from the table, he backed into another crewmember.

"Outta my way, pantywaist," grumbled soldier. Stalsius lurched one way and then another to avoid the growing crowd of ship hands. He was afraid and as he backed further into the crowd, he found himself panicking again and the world about His retreat led him all the way back into the heated serving area where Oteph stood, mindlessly slopping away with his military regulation spoon and oversized yellow spatula. " greasy brown apron was strapped across his chest and flowed down toward his waist.

"Well, look who crawled out of a rat-hole, It's prince what's-his-name." Stalsius wore an expression of deep shock as he saw and heard from a man that he had once admired. Stalsius trembled and felt his face burn with embarrassment as he stood before Oteph and the ever-increasing line of hungry crew. Oteph paused in mid-slop and looked carefully at the prince

"You better get some food; you look tired. Get it from Wendy.

Wendy was the cook's second mate and, unlike her senior, was always cleanly dressed. Stalsius thought it was the result of a lifetime of serving up mayonnaise and white sauce, but it was just her way. Soon he had been given enough food to last a few more days or perhaps a week if he was careful.

"Be sure and come back," Oteph called after him, "The guys all miss you." Oteph knew his comment was untrue and yet to him the power of the snide remark was so deeply ingrained that he felt he couldn't do anything but say things that were meant to hurt. He might just as well have said: "Relieve us, mighty prince, your presence is too potent for us."

Stalsius stumbled out the double doors laced his doublet and tied it straight an then made a slow deliberate return to his quarters. That night he gorged on the food he had gotten and with a full stomach he began to tend to his hygiene .

Oteph saw himself staying aboard the Freiheit for a year, the time it took to travel from the royal outpost on Ng to the low-tech world of Saurus. Space flight was not without excitement, though. While crossing the nexus, the Freiheit was for a short time captured and pillaged by pirates. Oteph, as cook, had little to do with any of it until the boarding party desired to relieve the galley of its fresh water and food supply. During a regular mealtime session when Oteph served as swiftly as a high-speed robot, the attacks came. First, the galley was flooded with light and under the brightness slipped a dozen men all armed to the teeth with concussion helmets, distraction rays and small brass knives. The crew were taken aback for a moment as they observed the scene. Oteph, himself, stopped serving, dropped his spoon and spatula and drew his force whip, but there was little he could do as the invaders soon overpowered the unarmed diners. Seeing a gap in the light, Oteph walked towards the corridor where he saw Stalsius ambling down to the galley in his usual tentative, tenuous manner.

"Get down, prince," he yelled, but Stalsius only paused to look about him and, seeing nothing, continued on his slow, dejected and unmusical way. Oteph was horrified to see an attacker creep up beside the prince and slide a long silver blade into Stalsius' cotton doublet and flowing blouse.

"No! Stop," Oteph shouted. But he was too late. The invader had wounded the prince seriously and as Stalsius slumped to the floor, Oteph was filled with rage. Placing his fingers on the bloodied shirt and the flowing wound beneath it, Oteph held Stalsius in his arms

"Say not that you have fallen." In the sequenced images, Oteph couldn't believe his eyes as he saw his dream self helping the shrinking violet of a man. Stalsius looked equally surprised. The formerly brutish cook had turned soft at the sight of his misfortune. Stalsius' body grew limp as he feinted for loss of blood. After carrying Stalsius to the med bay, Oteph applied a stimp pack to the gaping wound, wiped his own fingers of the prince' bright red blood and returned to the corridors where a much larger conflict had ensued, Regularly employed security and planet troops fought a losing battle against the much better armed invaders. The situation was hopeless, but Oteph drew on his natural meanness for a solution. With the force whip in one hand and his other stretched out to balance his ungainly body, he went on the attack. The force whip could bind, wound or even lacerate foes depending on its aspect and usage. Oteph was able to bind and shock up to two troopers at one time.

"long, heated boredom engulfed the small freighter as the regular spacers tried desperately to regain control over the Freiheit and expel the pirates. Oteph had long since left the galley and had taken up a strategic position amidships where his large round body rested against the forward pylon of the medical bay where Stalsius still lay, weak and delirious from the wound that had only just started to open again.

Oteph smartly kept an eagle's gaze over the medical bay as he sought, now from long distance to wound or render impotent the invaders. But now the tide had begun to turn. The crew had dropped their meals rushed back to their stations and, with the help of the formerly languid royals, had begun to beat the unwelcome guests back to the airlock. Oteph wondered at the unexpected usefulness of the royals who, at the sight of danger, dropped their colored robes and produced thin sharp blades that were comical in size and shape but used by them became deadly. Could Stalsius be one of these royal heroes, he thought to himself. One look back to the place where he came and he panicked. Stalsius had slipped away again.

Oteph had always seen royals the way that the rest of the world saw them-as weakened, dainty, girlish men and self-important ladies, but the incident on the Freiheit did much to change his thing. Underneath their silken robes and within their festive royal array, they carried the skill of expert soldiers. With knives as small as fresh sprout of a tree branch, they could overpower the attack of a massive brutish villain. Oteph, watching from the safety of the medical bay watched as the princes and ladies slowly took the battle away from the pirates by luring them back into the bridge past the stateroom. Slowly, one by one, the future leaders of Saurus moved silently from their chambers amidships. Fully trained in courtly battle, such royals rarely had the need to use them in real life. But this day was somehow different. It was surreal and yet it felt nice to them. The royal travelers moved quietly and with daggers made of gold awaited their prey. Courtly battle the computer, engineering and console controls. The royals slipped back to their rooms as quietly as they had come forth, most of them showing little signs of exercise.

Oteph turned to face Stalsius as he lay unconscious on the table. With what little medical knowledge he had, Oteph rifled through the cupboards and containers desperately searching for something to stanch the bleeding. Unsuccessfully, he only wound up making a mess of a formerly tidy room. Just then, captain Wiggins, commander of the health and well-being unit arrived to find the embarrassed, fearful Oteph holding handfuls of medical dressings from small gauze strips to instant heat packs. "t the sight of the Captain, he dropped everything on the floor.

"What are you doing to this prince?" He demanded. "I'm calling security."

"This man needs several stimp packs, but I can't find them," Oteph protested.

"He needs that, it's true, but you need out of here." It did not take long for the keenly dressed security patrol to appear at the door of the medical bay.

"Take this savage out of here and don't let him loose again. He has killed our great prince." The men strong-armed Oteph into a pair of strong binders and forced him to leave the room.

He needs medicine. I can help," Oteph yelled back towards the medical bay.

The medical captain cursed to himself as he looked down at Stalsius who had now drawn close to the very threshold of death.

How do pigs like that ever get aboard," he muttered, "Oh, well you wouldn't know."

Oteph was held in confinement for the rest of the journey. Branded as a thief and murderer, he was banished from Saurus and remained aboard the Freiheit only as long as he could find a system that could excuse his criminal past. But the time aboard the Freiheit changed him. With Stalsius as a friend, he had the chance of a new life as an acceptable, healthy member of the society of space. As a murderer, his was a life that was once again cursed to being planet bound on a remote system with little or no civilized society. He soon forgot the ways of the gentry making himself content t to lay in wait for yet another foray among society. After all, here on a new system no one cared about royalty because there was none. Saurus was primitive, backward and at the same time unhealthy. Oteph began a new life quickly. The rudimentary star port on the planet where he lived was only serviceable to small pods and the all terrain vehicles that they carried. Getting aboard would not be easy. Oteph still carried the force whip that had saved him from many troubles in the past, but somehow his strength failed him. The royals were a people tougher in fighting than anyone or anything he had ever seen, but when provoked they were silent an d deadly warriors. This appealed to Oteph and he thought of it each time he coiled up the 6 foot whip and replaced it at his side. To pick a fight was easy. To enjoin quietness was something he knew nothing about.

Oteph suddenly awoke to the feeling of a sharp boot slamming against his side. It seemed like days had passed since he fell asleep Under the overhang. What little shadows there were did not protect him from the afternoon rays of the bright sun. His skin ached from severe burns and blisters welled up on the tender skin of his face. As his eyes adjusted to the bright light he saw a huge personage towering above him. To his amazement, the person wore the lavender of Saurus and the broach of the king binding her cloak around herself. It was a princess of the realm.

"Stalsius said I might find you here," she said in a voice that was barely discernible from the warm wind, "I had my chance to kill you and I could have done so easily."

Oteph, parched from the extreme heat and lack of heat was speechless. "princess on a forbidden planet, he wondered.

"You must be far from home," He gasped, "Who came with you to keep you safe?"

"No one. I trust not in the affairs of men and machines."

The woman stepped back a few paces until she stood in the direct sunlight. The light shimmered as it hit her broach and the wind blew through her hair creating a rippling effect that was not unlike the waves of an ocean. But what ocean was this, he wondered. Her flowing lavender robe brushed against the hot stones

"Take me with you," Oteph said as he struggled to his feet, arms and legs aching from the run-in with the spiders.

"Suit yourself. You may not like what you see."

Oteph looked at her and noticed something that he hadn't seen before. Her face was marred by a scar that ran from her left eyelid to the base of her cheek. It was old wound, he thought, because the scar was not red but an imperceptible pink color.

"You've seen action," he said. The woman turned and walked away from him indicating that he should follow. For miles they walked with nothing in view except the hot unforgiving sun.

"How do you keep cool in such a cloak," he called after the princess but was greeted only by a quickened pace. Oteph struggled under the heat. His large fat body could not repel the heat and was unable to keep pace with the princess' long strides that eventually led them to the star port.

"You see, man," she said as she pointed to a large tracked vehicle, "This is how we intend to punish you."

After slowly lumbering aboard the ATV, Oteph looked around in wonder at an electronic wonderland filled with dimly lit consoles and pulsating orbs. Such equipment rarely appeared in the most advanced of the ships of the Saurian navy. Oteph paused to catch his breath. The atmosphere in the vehicle was hot and thick. Even a farmer like himself could become ill from such poisonous air

"What're you waiting for?" He heard a voice in the distance calling, "This is the way." Oteph was caught by the arm and dragged upward through the corridors of the massive machine. Oteph felt the darkness of nether regions turn to blazing light that seemed to burn his eyes even when he closed them. He was shoved forward and summarily crumpled to the floor.

""rise, tiny one and meet thy doom." " familiar voice chanted a threat that felt as pleasant as a prayer, All these years have brought strife. You, old friend, have killed our culture."

"But who are you, man?" Oteph implored.

"I am no man," and after saying this, the man stepped forward into view. It was prince Stalsius. Oteph looked at his old friend. His once angelic features were now care-worn, his eyes darkened and he could only see white cataracts where once beaming eyes shone forth the pride of his kingdom. " bent crown on his enfeebled head and a matted laurel adorned the upper corner of his lavender robe.

"Hello, old friend."

Twenty five

Oteph shrunk away in horror. Was this Stalsius? The seeming madman that had trusted the old pirate when he was hated by every corner of the galaxy?

"I guess it is...you," Oteph muttered.

"My friend," Stalsius rasped, "You are scheduled to be executed, for I am Stalsius the Great and it is believed that you tried to kill me. I'm sorry. It's out of my hands now. Old friend" Oteph noticed the wizened face of his old friend. Time and travel had worn away the youthful joviality that Oteph had once wondered at during his year-long mission aboard. Time had separated them, but the energy of the years in exile seemed to fall away like the scales of a long dried ocean fish.

"Uh... No hard feelings then?" Oteph murmured as if he expected to be struck down.

"It's not I that you should fear" Stalsius continued, " but my subjects. Farmers don't make kings and neither do notorious villains to which categories you both belong."

"The lady...Who is she?"

"Anissah," he continued, "My royal Paige. She will transmit us back to the Capital where you will be tried and I will look with on with no small interest." Oteph drummed his fingers on a nearby console. It was a nervous tick that he had, but in this case, the lights of the bridge turned on and lights flashed around the chamber.

"Oh, I should have reminded you. This is not a tractor." Oteph was slack-jawed. On the outside, the mechanical beast looked like an ordinary pulling tractor, but on the inside it was quite otherworldly.

"But it runs on two feet?" Oteph asked, almost afraid of the answer.

"Six points, actually. Electro kinesthetics," Anissah answered

"Oh... How obvious," Oteph concurred, "How stupid of me." Indeed the craft did seem to float effortlessly above the crude rocky ground of the plain where Anissah had intercepted him and drawn him into the beastly machine. Oteph scratched around in the parched dirt to see if any life still dwelt beneath the upper soil.

"You're right," Stalsius commented, "It has all been sterilized by a catastrophe that occurred long ago. The still times."

"You talk as if you were there."

"I was there... and so were you" Stalsius' face no longer beamed with positivity, but instead his countenance became that of one who was possessed by a perhaps evil spirit. Stalsius' body grew completely rigid and he attempted to steady himself by grabbing the side of a console guarding bar. In spite of his best efforts, he slumped to the ground and grunted softly before laying still on the floor.

"Great," Oteph muttered, "Now this and now that." Oteph gave Stalsius a few tentative kicks in the ribs to make sure that he was still unconscious. Oteph gazed about the self-starting bridge with wonder. Anissah was right, this was no tractor; it was a marvelous sight. What a simpleton she must think of him. While Oteph obsessed about his lack of culture, he was shoved back into an operator's chair.

"You must be kidding," he grumbled, "You can't expect me to fly this machine."

"Of course not," Anissah purred, "You will communicate with it ."

Oteph felt strange sensations as he strapped himself into the anti-seizure cuffs. After placing a mouth guard firmly between his teeth and fitting a leather-like binding across his forehead, Anissah took one last satisfied look at her prey and made several inaudible commands to Stalsius. The last thing he remembered was the feel of burning eye drops that were applied to his eyes between forced-open eyelids.

"I feel refreshed," he said as he looked with unusual clarity at peaceful murals painted on the walls of what seemed to be the study of a large manor house. In spite of his talking no one answered except for the gentle scented breeze of freshly cut grass an d flowering shrubs.

"Where am I?" he asked almost involuntarily.

"You're home, Oteph. I'm surprised you didn't recognize it." Stalsius was out of his robe wearing just a lavender tunic and flared pants as he looked to the place where Oteph sat. "You've survived a great deal. All in all, I'd say you were a miracle waiting to happen."

"Legs! Where are my legs!" Oteph cried as he grasped the chair where he sat.

"They are where you left them," Anissah answered.

And where is that, pray?" Oteph asked.

"They are on Saurus, primary planet of Homunculus system./ You're home. Your home," Anissah answered without showing any regard for Oteph's ever-increasing panic. Oteph remained silent as he tried to reach for his legs and other body parts. They were gone. His legs, once perfect specimens of human laziness had been replace, at least superficially, with a hard rubber substance that seemed to be drawn tight over the surface of a hard but completely fluid mass. Moving them required effort and mental focus and it was weeks until he could manipulate his knee joint and later his new hip joint. Anissah and Stalsius became better friends than he had ever known.

Anissah was prone to fits of bitchiness which she adequately concealed with her natural free spirit and won the hearts of the two men just as quickly as she had lost them to some negative or vituperative thought.

Oteph progress very slowly and it was indeed months until Stalsius told him why he was taken from Saurus and transported to the royal outpost.

"You see, it's just that we could not leave you in the hands of the people."

"And my legs?"

"That was our mistake perhaps. We tried to reconstruct your body until it matched the profile of the one you had at the beginning of the Freiheit. On that ship your leg rotted away from gangrene."

"So you put these candy wrappers on me," Oteph said with rising anger. "I know what I should have done with you..."

Stalsius was taken aback The comment had stopped him cold. It was true that the obese farmer-turned had been there for him at that critical moment. They both looked at each other as they saw Anissah approaching.

"Step aside, you pigs," she hissed, "Better yet. Beat it"

"We didn't mean nothin'" Oteph pleaded.

"You were talking and you should be especially ashamed."

Unfortunately, Oteph did not understand or feel the anger in her voice.

"Yes," he said in an almost robotic tone , "friend Stalsius. Friend Anissah."

"I think I'm living in the stone ages with a couple of sub-sapients. Oteph looked on as though he had fallen asleep while Stalsius looked at Anissah as if to allay her fears about the two men.

"We're not that bad once you get to know us."

"And who are you?" Anissah's question stung deeply. After all, Oteph was a robotically enhanced human mind contained within a shell of hardened rubber while Stalsius was a deeply scarred prince of the realm who was once saved from death by the quick actions of a cook. Stalsius stopped talking and as he looked at the beastly pirate, he seemed to feel a new sympathy for him. How was it that a miserable farmer could even dream of the stars rather than his next serving of gruel. Stalsius had always lived on the outpost with friends his age and of equal wealth and influence. Now that he was king, he thought he had the right to shape men's lives by the flick of his finger. True, Oteph was a sad piece of work and fully deserved to be dismembered by the crew on the Freiheit, but this common criminal still possessed the base instinct of saving the lives of those he thought profitable.

"Who cares," Oteph would have said, "I hate those pantywaists anyway. The can bump themselves off for all I care. And their weapons... they're not even worth talking about." Oteph was a living breathing center of confusion. He hated most things in life except his own private pleasures, the ability to offend those of high degree and to arouse a genuine sense of revulsion among those whom he thought deserving. Oteph sat and smiled to himself while he thought to himself about his next actions.

"Just look at you," Stalsius said in a mocking tone, "Not only do you fail to suffer at the loss of your body, but you grin and chortle besides. Crazy."

Oteph was alone in a world of his own making. With fondness, he remembered the ill-suited kweegons whose innocent trust he had soon exploited not long after their leader taught him to fly. The kweegons. Where did they go, he wondered. He rubbed his plastic fingers once more against the firm hide that now stretched across his newly-made legs. As he watched Stalsius and Anissah walk into the darkness of the night, he followed also, until the sheer weight of his body became too heavy for his own legs to support and he slumped to the ground as limp as a de-boned tractator. Gradually, walking became second nature to him and he learned to run and shoot weapons just as he had done at the peak of his career. Anissah found pleasure in watching him improve while Stalsius grow green with his apparent lack of relevance.

"Listen," he had said, "I don't know what happened, but it's not cool. You and Stal. Cut it out."

"Pathetic words coming from a mean who can't even raise his miserable body from the dirt of the ground. The insult hurt Oteph to the core. " woman he thought he almost liked before she took Stalsius from him. Days would pass until Stalsius would notice him as he sat on a metal chair in the twilight of the hours of sunset. Stalsius grew older, but never more full of life when he chose to visit his friend.

"I do like you Ot.' It's Anissah. She wants to build a friendship that goes beyond the confines of the lab in which I live."

What he said was true. King Stalsius became among things, the professor of science and evolutionary design He literally projected the future of the race of the

Saurians while reconstructing the past of a planet long overcome in the technology of its neighboring system, the Andilax and even more so in the case of the highly developed Xerxians.

"You deserve to be king," Oteph said in a voice that almost resembled words of love or poetry. Oteph had begun to change since the operation and the concomitant painful therapy and voice training. Such retraining was necessary after his descent into the criminal world after "attempting to kill his majesty the king." The very sound of his offense was enough to curdle the blood of any patriotic or otherwise plebeian soul in polite society.

"I deserve to be the devil. I watched them cut your arms and legs off and replace them with these blackened stumps. 'Is this what they call reintegration? Cybernetic superiority?' Who invented that if was not those blasted chumps from Andilax." It was true that Stalsius had worked hard to overcome the slowness of thought that was the blessing and curse of his people, but interference by other species in what he thought to be the business of the king was hateful to him. The influence of superior cultures such as the telepathic Andilaxians and the intellectually mysterious Xerxians lay far beyond the ken of the Saurian mind and yet there was a kind of hero worship among the people toward anyone who had ever experienced the high tech cultures. Stalsius and Oteph were among the affected few

Stalsius preferred the sterile silence of the lab to the pretense and pomp of the court. He preferred the feeling of the decaying leather apron across his middle to the full regalia of a Saurian king: the cape, sword, sash and the crown of purest iridium.

Anissah, too, preferred the lab to facing a sometimes cold and confusing world. The results of testing a substance in the microcosm of a test tube was more real than the neighbor that worked incessantly at his lawn across the street from the department of developmental evolution.

During a time when Oteph began to walk without a cane and the plastic legs were no longer a mystery to him, Anissah sat with Stalsius in his open court. The thoughts on their minds were predictable, but then crudely obvious. She loved the king! Oteph panicked and then cultivated a deep hatred in himself for the

Stalsius needed a queen, Oteph concluded. Perhaps he was sitting there under the sun asking her about that very subject. After all, he thought, Anissah was the closest example of a true female friend that he had known since arriving home and going through the perfunctory steps of being anointed and crowned.

Oteph watched the coronation on the video screen with disbelief and a generally sour disposition. Anissah was equally uninspired and Stalsius simply groaned as the prime mover placed the uncomfortable and heavy crown on top of his head. In his kingly splendor, "Anissah noticed his beauty as something she had never seen before. Stalsius was noble, handsome and fierce and it warmed her heart to see him thus.

Anissah sought that familiarity of heart in a man that would engender hope, security and the happiness that is akin to a life of blessed wisdom meted out with genuine episodes of pure love. The thing that was unhappily missing in the riches and fame the court.

"My first duty," muttered Stalsius, "is to rid myself of this tiresome formality." Stalsius flung his crystal sword across the royal chamber and listened to the high-pitched skittering sound it made as it bounced off of the crystalline floor.

"But," an elderly Paige said, "They have saved you in the past."

"Nay. I say not that they or any other form of courtly combat saved any one person aboard that ship. Or anywhere, anytime toward anyone."

Oteph realized the reference to the journey of the Freiheit from Ng to the planet Saurus. Twenty royal wards armed with only ceremonial thorn-knives had overcome an entire band of armed pirates.

"No! You don't know what you're saying. It was perhaps the silliness of those small weapons that regained the ship."   In his mind's eye, he saw himself escaping from the duties of a potentate and rushing toward the enjoyment of a day spent in the lab with Anissah. That was freedom. Freedom from a world of annoyances and pretensions of the courtly lifestyle.

As Stalsius grew into the role of the king and Anissah, his princess followed, too, he ordained Controller Otephus Black, the hated one, took the position of Protector of the Commonwealth. In his role as Controller, Oteph a supervised only trade activities in and out of Saurus, but in the Protectorate, he became the controller all of the visitations and the overseer of the cultural riches. Imagine, he thought. Me! a cultural protector! I who has shunned a thousand niceties, spit in the face of decency and destroyed lives and world with the determined slash of a whip.

Stalsius' overthrow was complete. Oteph was no longer a beast, but a man of responsibility, character, love and devotion. He began to bathe, shave his face and cultivate a clean manner and a soft voice. But he hesitated as he thought of the days gone by. The once hated aliens: the Asunur, the walking spiders and the ant-like creatures known only to inhabit the wastelands.

Soon, travelers from as far away as Xerxus came to Saurus with cultural trade to buy and sell. The kweegons, Thaulab, Tuvalo and Bo'agg arrived to create a moistened atmosphere in the Northern regions of the planet. The South was also modified to leave only the meridian height of equatorial Saurus to the ever-increasing Asunur. Chief Agwentuli took his well-deserved place as Governor General while king and queen grew old with age.

Thaulab approached the throne of his old friend Otephus with careful but determined steps.

"Our relations have changed, I see."

"Not so much as you might think, my friend," Oteph replied, "Saurus needs you just as they need the Asunur. We are a needy, childlike

people."

"Nay, I would say that you had learned your lesson well. I have instilled the hive in your Northern regions so that Saurus will never want water or moisture again. Your farms will flourish and the land will bloom once more. Spring is coming."

Twenty six

The Iraarku were a tribe of dark-haired natives that had found shelter in the communities of the borderlands. Long despised by their neighbors the Igoilenat. Their hawk-like features made them stand apart from the plain-featured Zapab. Oteph sat with his hands tied in cords and joined with similar bindings around his waist, knees and neck. His huge size created a puzzle for them. His knee bindings were supposed to be waist locks and the ankle locks that squeezed his legs into numbness were intended for the knees of a normally apportioned humanoid. Oteph chortled to himself and once again gloried in the size of his fatness. He was soon to be witness to a sight that made savagery all the more pleasant to him. "young family of Igoilenat had been caught in the streets, and, if his understanding of the primitive tongue was accurate, had presented the Iraarku with the personal insult of stopping and eating a meal. "young warrior was called before the moot and, with pride and happiness in his gait and stance, told of his heroic capture of the "devil breeders." "hush fell over the crowd as he told of the harrowing episode in which he captured the small boy while combating the ferocious sister. The crowd gasped with awe and fright as he showed them fingernail scratches and tooth indentations on his forearms. "guilty verdict was struck immediately and the mother and her children were burned alive in the city square. The fires of the judgment illuminated the park long into the evening. The charred bodies of the family were hoisted high over the streets of the city as a warning to any other breeders that might think of living in the Iraarku world. As Oteph looked at these things he was reminded of the Hive and its children. Children he would never see again. After all, Thaulab gave this old pirate several chances to change that which was unchangeable, and yet, there was no way of becoming so deeply spiritual as to become any use to the Hive and its relations. He held his head in both hands in an unsuccessful bid to drive away the shame that he knew he deserved.

Oteph was once again stripped of his possessions, bound at the knees, waist and arms and left in a bare yard that consisted of three walls composed of dry timbers, a pot for defecation and a bowl for slop. "bout his neck, a rough collar had been fitted that prevented him from wandering outside the demesne of the yard. for rest there was a bed of mud and a three-legged stool.

"You did this to me, Thaulab," he muttered under his breath.

"Nobody to save you this time, friend," said a passerby, "your 'friends' dropped off this." The man, obviously a desert dweller. dropped his elaborate flag, a few broken hammers and three small knives. Nice friends you've got."

Oteph looked up with hatred in his heart. He glowered at his captors but not nearly as much as he raged inwardly toward Thaulab. If he caught them, he would tear them into so many pieces that even the Hive could not fix them. Yes, he knew of their weaknesses and he immediately set to work on a new plan. In between foul tasting mouthfuls of pig fodder, he flexed his muscles against his strong bindings to convince himself of their existence. He repeated this action every hour and half-hour and it comforted him, allowing him to think and plot. Hateful feelings toward the original visitors were not answered as they had been in the past and, as time wore on , he felt himself happily liberated from the Hive which he increasingly considered to be a spot of evil in the universe. They had come to destroy the Igoilenat, a stupid people, yes, but what about the beginnings of life?. Oteph had seen their young clinging to their mothers in foolish trust of a life that would now be taken. He saw them slaughtered and their tiny bodies ripped apart by visitors who came to destroy an entire race.

Oteph was beyond thinking evil now. He sought a way to escape from his prison and strike back at the evil ones. It was not to be because months passed before he was visited with an opportune time. One of his captors demanded him to come close the rail that divided him from the free and open world. It was a tooth check. " tiny, swarthy man in a leather coat thrust his fingers into Oteph's mouth. Probing every tooth and gum, the man whistled for a much stronger man who jerked Oteph out of the cell and laid him supine on the floor. From there he could see the sun as it reared its bright head far above the eastern horizon. He hadn't seen the bright star for a long time and now its countenance astonished him as if its shining was a miracle in the sky.

Such occurrences were rare and Oteph lived his days as a beast would. He grew ferocious at feeding times and raged against bindings at others. Children passed his pen and threw rocks or clods of dirt at him. This he hated more than everything and the pain of it caused him to stay in certain areas of the yard that were not reachable by mockers and the endless clods of dirt and dried animal feces.

Oteph learned that the food of a prisoner was mostly chunks of raw animal fat, gristle and tripe. His formerly impressive form dwindled and his size and strength decreased to the extreme. He was no longer large and corpulent but lean, wiry and, on some occasions, rather spry. He was fed by a keeper that threw great rocks at him before pouring out a plate of foul smelling slop . He often glared at him but then comforted himself with lustful ideas about what he would do in return . Months on the diet of an Iraarku slave made him weak and as he was compelled to live with discipline, his body and mind grew strong once more. He would kill his captors

The time came for his release on a rainy day when mud and slop rose and mixed together. Standing barefoot in the mess, Oteph watched as his persecutor arrived with a key to the pen. Springing quickly upon the guard, he shattered his leg with the side of the metal slop plate. Pig food covered the guard as he thrashed on the ground in bloody pain. Oteph took the ring of keys and the tunic from the guard. So many days without clothes made the fabric feel very strange and unnatural as he realized that the desert dwellers wore nothing save a belt to hold stones and a sling. "t times he would view the equivalent of a pack animal. They were large over-fed ogres, much like him, that balanced huge loads of food, equipment and weapons on their backs. Every morning they went out and every evening they came back with new supplies, more food and more captives. Today's catch was a small family of Igoilenat that had strayed too close to the town center. They were immediately spotted, bound and tied to a beast. The older pair simply trudged through the gate and collapsed in the mud.

Oteph felt sorry for them. Poor miserable scum. Even they deserved a better fate than this. They would die here. They would die like pigs. Oteph felt stirrings in the vacuous hole that used to be his heart. Mothers an d theirs babies were kicked and spat upon and then were force fed the ubiquitous. Needless to say, the children languished on it, fathers and mothers vomited most of it up. After a while, a great host of Igoilenat lay in perpetual imprisonment.

The time came for his release on a rainy day when mud and slop rose and mixed together. Standing barefoot in the mess, Oteph watched as his persecutor arrived with a key to the pen. Springing quickly upon the guard, he shattered his leg with the side of the metal slop plate. Pig food covered the guard as he thrashed on the ground in bloody pain. Oteph took the ring of keys and the tunic from the guard. So many days without clothes made the fabric feel very strange and unnatural as he realized that the desert dwellers wore nothing save a belt to hold stones and a sling. "t times he would view the equivalent of a pack animal. They were large over-fed ogres, much like him, that balanced huge loads of food, equipment and weapons on their backs. Every morning they went out and every evening they came back with new supplies, more food and more captives. Today's catch was a small family of Igoilenat that had strayed too close to the town center. They were immediately spotted, bound and tied to a beast. The older pair simply trudged through the gate and collapsed in the mud.

So t his was the great super race. The one that he had hoped to rob, rape and pillage. Oteph saw to it that he never watched the creatures in their sickening efforts at keeping clean. There was no way. Dirt, filth and excrement covered every corner of the pens where the Igoilenat were herded. Oteph was lucky enough to be an outsider. The Iraarku had noted his strength and dangerous abilities so here he sat unfettered by the filth and stink of a people slowly dying the death of a conquered race. Home was slipping fast from the civilized era of science and law to the fractious thrum of the tribal era. Oteph smiled. I'm home, he thought.

After his first incident with the keeper, Oteph had been allowed free access to all parts of the encampment. His lithe body strolled up and down the lee ways along the pens and he watched the poor creatures as they eked out a miserable imprisonment. Despite the scenes of outright need, Oteph despised the creatures in his heart as he did all things that weren't of personal interest to him. " child lifted its tiny arms to him in hopes of a hand out. He picked up a large rock and cast it at the child who's face gushed with blood as he cried out in agony.

"You waste my time, I'll waste yours."

"young woman, obviously the parent and giant with the approach of yet another of her species said, "You pig bastard of a man. You above all should know better." She held the sobbing child in her arms as bright blood flowed. Oteph regarded the mother and moved on silently. Oteph became tired of himself. Having a new body didn't change him and he didn't know what would. Perhaps being free of the pen had crippled him

"You're lucky to live in that crap," he said at one occasion to a group of besotted prisoners. Now he realized only too well what his mocking words really meant. It was the old contempt breeds honesty breeds contempt minus ego equals contempt in the giver or something to that effect. He couldn't remember the phrase. He hated remembering, hated learning anything and hated the world. It was a sunny and delightful occasion when Oteph looked down on the fugitives and looked up to his original captors. He would become a tribesman, a real Iraarku.

Ukkmudaku-Oteph spent the first days of his new life being carved and tattooed by shaman spiritists of the higher order. It was a new life for him, but one that would further distance himself from a life of cruel selfishness and violence of his past. The Iraarku were a peaceful people at heart and so he realized that he must like them or rejoin the ranks of the captives, the Igoilenat, eating dung off the ground and drinking foul water, if it could be called that, from the waste buckets. For the first time, Ukkmadaku felt the ease of knowing the structure of life. He was a base warrior. His comrades, the spirit listeners, and his denizen s the captive miserable ones

Clan life was as simple as the daily life of a sub servant consisted mainly of laying around and sunning oneself in the sand dunes that covered the once bustling streets and alley ways of the city. Normally only spiders and their masters traveled through these places, but Ukkmadaku often wandered away deeper into town to see the approach of more prisoners or to bake in the on the sand in the heat of the day. The latter instance was his most common reason for visiting the city.

The town was washed out, sandblasted and bleached by several years of increasing sand storms that arrived by the superheated winds from the wastelands. Ukkmadaku gazed deeply onto the sun and felt the shimmering effect that one feels after looking directly into an object of unhealthy brightness. He no longer cared. Let them come, he thought to himself. One people dies another feeds on its carcass. So goes the glory of the world. "and yet here too, he is going away. He had accepted Home as a place for himself too long. Then he set out again to find Saurus, his home.

The expedition left that morning. forty-four spiders laden with their masters and boxes of chains, stones and spears jingled as the train of Iraarku trudged through the murky sandy streets. Ukkmadaku watched as the spiders marched out in rows of two, the final section forming a diamond shape of four larger ones to hold supplies for the journey. He was assigned to the rear of the column to watch over food stuffs while those senior to him scanned the horizon and policed empty building for the presence of what they called the "miscreants." The hot brazen sun and the whipping sand soon got to Ukkmadaku. He raised a dirty finger to his eye to wipe away particles of sand. Failing to win the war against the small irritations, he fashioned his scarf into a facemask that covered all except a small place on his face for sight. He was largely despised by his fellow marauders because of his lengthy stay in the pens. His reputation as an impudent, immature bully marked him as untrustworthy.

Ukkmadaku-Oteph's mount was slowed by his weight and that of countless pounds of metal weapons. While other spiders could stand tall enough for their masters to see into the higher levels of buildings, his was lucky to amble forward on the uncertain ground of the city. What a sight it made. "humbled space villain sitting in a most unflattering way while real heroes made a straight course toward a goal that would be rewarded at its completion. He felt the pain of hunger and would gladly have broken into the food stuffs that he was entrusted with, but he knew the peril of such an act. He put it out of his mind and sallied forward through the dust.

As the day wore on and Ukkmadaku grew delirious from hunger and dehydration, he felt first his head floating and then his entire body fall away from him as he collapsed into the dust. The spider stopped for a minute, puzzled, and then carried on without him. Ukkmadaku felt himself drift away only to be awakened by the clanking of metal bars being fastened around his wrists and secured to his back. He was firmly secured onto the back of a spider and, as he looked about, saw that he was fettered like a great host of the enemy of whom some were carried like him and thousands of others who were tied together on foot behind the procession. The day had vanished and darkness had surrounded the city. The spiders knew where they were going. Day by day, it was always to the same location- a wide sandy field in the oldest part of the town. In the language, it was called simply "common" and was used as they meeting place with all other tribes. The landscape teemed with spiders, men and shiny personages. Once again, the central location was illuminated by the presence of a luminous object that Ukkmadaku could only make out as the glowing personage of a woman, unclothed, looking over the field. The clicking and scuffling of feet hushed as the image grew larger and brighter. Ukkmadaku could feel his mount lowering itself to the ground as if to show a kind of filial homage.

The long night consisted of watching rows and rows of spiders and their riders coming close to the bright image, basking awhile in her heated gaze and then returning to the rear of the formation. It came to be the turn of the Iraarku just as Ukkmadaku had satisfied himself that all motion had stopped the evening. Having been rifling through the contents of the foodstuffs, he was rudely interrupted by the sharp poke of a spear underneath his chin.

"Hey, fatso, lay off," they said, "not yours anyway." Ukkmadaku could feel a wave of guilt and humility flowing over him. He owed his new life to the Iraarku people and, in his shame, forgot what he was. He averted his eyes from the group even they approached the place where the personage stood. "t that time, he felt electrified by the moment. The woman's look caused blindness and joy to fill his heart. The feeling of raw energy coursed through his lifeblood and seemed to make him stronger. The presence seemed to have a similar effect on his newfound brothers, the Iraarku. Electricity leaped from one warrior to another and as it lay only but a moment each of them stood taller in their mounts and seemed to hold their spears in profound ways. Such was not the knowledge of Home nor its inhabitants. Even the long -reigning Igoilenat had no record of the energy that flowed so freely from a geographical locale. Ukkmadaku wondered if similar places existed in all of the badlands and forbidden areas. There was an unseen power here and he wanted it. In the months following his acceptation into the tribes of the Iraarku, the previously named Oteph grew in favor with his new people who would have had him as their chieftain if not for his dishonesty and stealing of food.

Daily, he rummaged through trash bins, empty eating halls and just-used dishwashers for any scraps of tasty food. He had long since regained his portly figure and was now the strong large man that he was before, trailing into battle like the mightiest of weapons that could conquer any foe. This was Ukkmadaku, the well-apportioned one.

Twenty seven

The one called Comptroller Otephus Black slumbered in front of a factory security screen. The day was almost done, and his life was about to begin. Slipping into a ragged black cloak and binding its folds against his waist, he arranged the weapons of his trade against hi body. He was now the grand Protector and, as such, could ill afford to be without a means of defending those of the crown. He took more pride in his work for the royal party than he did his job for the Governor General who paid higher and rewarded him with notoriety and fame. King Stalsius could never do this. The royal family was as weak as the drive for space exploration under the Science Foundation.

It came only as a shock to find the old king in an alley-way picking about for food while trying to keep his lavender robe from touching the depressing greasy filth on the roadway.

"Time to get outta here, bums," Oteph snarled. The king, knowing his old friend, said plainly,

"I am at your mercy, wise one." Stalsius struggled to his feet and attempted to acknowledge the large security guard whose identity he did not know.

"You're wearing gold and iridium! Where did you steal it from?" Oteph snarled, "Such property belongs only to the king and his family. I shall have those and return them from whence they came.

The enfeebled Stalsius carefully removed the iridium buckles and golden binders that once signified him as the king and gave them to the Protector. Oteph weighed the objects carefully and mumbled to himself, "These were the property of Stalsius. How did you get them."

"I don't know," Stalsius croaked," I must have stolen them just like you said."

"No. That's too simple. Move into the light where I can see you. ""h, the king's garments al full of filth. What are you doing here, Stalsius, o king. Surely I deserve to dwell in this place, but not you. Your life dwells in fancy iridium chambers of court."

"No it doesn't" Stalsius replied, "My life belongs to the people I serve. That is why I am, as you say a 'bum'"

But your crown, you cannot leave it"

"No. I cannot," Stalsius' voice became quiet, "That is why I am giving it to you. Long may you rule Saurus and blessings be on your head should troubles ever arise." Stalsius produced the shiny crown that had once identified him as the leader of realm and defender of the Foundation.

"Take care of Anissah. She longs for you, Oteph." with that, the ancient king wheezed and lay softly back onto the wet pavement.